Neil Bailey was born in [obscured] and lives in Greenwich, L[obscured] *When She Was Bad,* was rel[obscured] in 2016 to five star reviews and was shortlisted for the 2018 *Write Here, Right Now* prize. The follow-up, *Bad For Good*, was published in 2017 and continued the adventures of Barclay and MacDonald.

Learn more about the author at
www.neilmbailey.com

The Woman at Twenty-six

Neil Bailey

Also by Neil Bailey, published by Dexter Kirby Press

When She Was Bad

Bad For Good

Barclay & MacDonald (omnibus edition)

COPYRIGHT

All characters and events in this publication, other than those clearly in the public domain, are fictitious and any resemblance to real persons, living or dead, is purely coincidental.

Copyright © 2018 Neil Martin Bailey

The moral right of the author has been asserted.

All rights reserved. No part of this publication may be reproduced, stored in a retrieval system, or transmitted, in any form or by any means, without the prior permission in writing of the author or publisher.

ISBN: 9781726729314

Cover design by Jenny Bailey
Cover image: Marc Pascual, courtesy of
www.pixabay.com

For Els

I.

I hated him from the moment his hand first touched mine.

Okay, as Beth would point out if she were still around, maybe "hate" is a little strong, but "didn't like" doesn't really say it and the macho, vice-like grip of his handshake crushed my fingers and immediately got my back up.

And besides, this is my story, not hers, so I'll stick with "hate".

There was something untrustworthy in that lying face; the way he couldn't hold eye contact with me, his hand constantly seeking the reassurance of his precious iPhone.

I should have realised then that this was wrong, especially when he kept calling me "mate" despite the fact I'd only known him for a few minutes. But Beth's excitement was infectious and I was swept along in its wake. I was just grateful to see her happy.

'Have many people seen it? Before us, I mean?' she asked.

The estate agent looked up from his wretched phone. 'I'm sorry?'

'Number twenty-four. Have you shown many people around?'

'It's a buyer's market,' he replied with a highly polished grin. 'We're very busy with every single property on our books at the moment. There's another couple scheduled to see this house at two so we'll have to be quick. Squeezing you in to a busy schedule on this one. It's a highly sought-after area.'

I was walking a few paces ahead, glancing at the tall terraced houses. 'You agents always say that,' I said. 'Part of the game we're playing. "It's a buyers' market." "Plenty of interest in this one." I bet the only customers you've got queueing around the block are in your dreams.'

The agent, whose name I had already forgotten, widened his grin. 'Mate, you couldn't be more wrong! The market's always really, really stellar at this time of year. Nature of the beast. Weather picks up and it's like a stone's been lifted and buyers want to get moving and make the most of it. It's that next right,' he said, nodding and waving his phone like he was directing invisible traffic.

'I like old houses,' Beth said. 'Just think of all the families that have lived here before. All those memories.'

'Early Victorian these,' said the agent. Was he Tom? Or was it Tim? Beth would remember. She was the one with the eye for detail. Just as well, as she was also going to be our family's money earner now, the one paying attention to the bank balance and our ability to afford this place. We had a few others on our list but she seemed to think this was the one and I wasn't going to disagree. It was the cheapest by far, and in a nice area, too.

'Early Victorian? What's that, 150 years' old? 200?' I didn't even get a GCSE in History at school and I'm a dead loss at the whole kings and queens business.

'Mid-19th century. These were all originally workers cottages for some engineering company down the road. The Smethwick factory got bombed in the war, direct hit during the Blitz. Long gone. They've built new apartments on that ground now. Nice but pricey, thanks to the amazing views. Worth going to have a look. Built for the City crowd and very popular with the overseas buyers. Sell a lot to the Chinese these days. And Russians. I prefer these places though. Those Victorians built property to last. More character. Charm. These houses have stood the test of time as you're about to see.' He was all clichés.

Beth chose to add one of her own: 'If the walls could talk, eh? They must have seen it all. Who knows what's happened behind these doors?'

The agent laughed his fakest laugh. 'Could be haunted,' he said. 'You believe in ghosts?' We both smiled, shaking our heads.

We took the next turning and I dropped back in step with my wife. I took her hand and gave it a squeeze as we turned into Amersham Place. She turned to me, her eyes bright. I hadn't seen her this excited in a long time. Her unpredictable mood swings and the tantrums of the pregnancy had exhausted us both and stretched our relationship to its limit at times.

No more. New beginnings and all that. And I was on my best behaviour.

Was this it? Our new street? Our first family home? A chance for happier times after all the strain of the last year? I looked up and the light summer puffs of white cloud parted right on cue and rays of sunshine made the rain-soaked street sparkle in greeting. Beth's eyes widened and she let out a sigh. She leaned closer to me. 'It's beautiful, Ben,' she breathed in my ear.

Maybe beautiful was pushing it – it was an East London street, old but hardly the stuff of poetry, more Dickens than Wordsworth. Two long terraces of narrow three and four storey houses, their bricks darkened by the years of pollution. The houses stood patiently to attention, shoulder to shoulder, as if awaiting inspection. Which, in a way, number twenty-four was.

'There are a lot of cars here, considering it's the weekend,' I said. 'Is parking a problem?'

'It's London,' said Tom (or Tim), as if that was answer enough.

'But parking?'

'There are annual residents' parking permits,' said the agent.

'So that's a "yes", then? Parking's a problem?'

'There it is!' interrupted Beth, pointing down the street. I followed her finger and saw the house we'd come to view. I was smiling, despite the agent's inability to give a straight answer to any of my questions.

The 'For Sale' sign picked it out from the others but as I approached I could see our seller had put in some extra effort to attract a buyer. Twenty-four's brickwork stood out. It had been recently cleaned of the city's grit and grime, making it look like a late arrival, newly built among its less pristine neighbours. Newly painted too. The woodwork and sills sparkled in their clean white gloss, the front door stern and solid in a rich, deep shiny scarlet, its chrome fittings polished and glinting.

Beth's stride quickened and she slipped her hand from my grip in her impatience. 'Not so fast,' I called after her.

But it was too late. Beth was already through the gate and striding purposefully up the short garden path.

'Bloody hell,' I said under my breath and I turned to the agent. Tom. It was definitely Tom.

'It's passed the Beth test then, Tom,' I said.

'Looks like it, mate,' said the agent. 'And it's Tim by the way.'

Of course it was. 'I best catch up with my wife.'

'You do that, mate,' said Tim.

I could have sworn he'd introduced himself as Tom. And if he called me 'mate' one more time, I was going to swing for him.

*

'When is the baby due?'

'Couple of months,' I said, unable to contain my grin. Tim couldn't have looked less interested but then it's probably second nature in his game to keep up a high level of small talk and chatter without really hearing a word. Anything was preferable to actually answering any of the customers' real concerns. 'Is that damp up there?'

'Just the light, I'm sure.' Tim wasn't even looking in the right direction. 'Mrs Collins liked the lounge then?'

I nodded. 'It looked newly decorated?'

'Yes. The seller chose to redecorate to encourage a quick sale. Not that he'll have to worry on that count. We've had a lot of interest already and it's only the first week.'

'Yeah, you said. You sure that's the light and not

some leak or something?'

'You'll be having a survey, I assume? They will highlight anything that needs attention. It's all newly decorated and there are warranties on all the work, appliances and everything.'

'Sure,' I said, unconvinced. It looked like a damp patch to me.

Beth's father had bored me stupid about warranties. 'Ain't worth the paper they're written on. I know. Been there, seen it myself a thousand times.' He had an opinion on everything, that man. He was another one who'd rubbed me up the wrong way from moment one and over the last year I'd had more than enough of arguing with him for one lifetime, thank you very much. Beth and I needed our own space and I didn't want our own child growing up anywhere near that man if I could find a way to avoid it.

I had to admit that twenty-four Amersham Place ticked enough of our boxes to make it a serious contender. The survey would determine if that was damp in the bedroom above the window, probably a blocked gutter or loose tile on the roof. Anything like that would help us knock a few thousand off the price.

Not that it was completely unaffordable, but every penny saved would help. Pretty cheap according to that website for the area Beth had found. 'Quick sale. Chap got transferred to his company's Scottish office last month,' was the explanation given for the low price when Beth had asked the agent about it. The seller, who I assumed we would never meet, had at least put the effort into making it look ready for someone to move into straight away. Maybe us?

'Have you seen out here?' Beth shouted from outside. I walked over to the bedroom window and peered below. The early summer sunshine was showing the garden at its best, a thin path of manicured green grass bordered by brightly leaved bushes, leading to a shed, nestling in the shadow of a mature apple tree that looked like it could soon be heavy with fruit. A shed! I had never had a shed to call my own before. Every man should have a shed.

Yes, it was all starting to look almost too good. Not perfect; nowhere ever would be, but this looked like it would be good for us. Of course, I wasn't a gardener by any stretch of the imagination, but there was precious little grass to mow and that paving out the front would probably just need a blast with a pressure washer every so often. That would be fun. I had always fancied having a go with one of those.

Beth gave another childish squeal from downstairs, some other new discovery, and for a second I felt a gentle tightness in my chest reminding me how much I had loved her. Maybe, in our new home, she might feel that way about me again, too.

'I think we should go down to the basement and check out the kitchen,' said Tim. 'We can't stay much longer as my colleague will be showing that other couple around shortly.'

I followed him down the steep stairwell. I tried the bannister with my left hand and it wobbled at my touch. 'That's a bit loose,' I said.

'Easily fixed mate,' said Tim. I wasn't so sure about that – I'm not exactly the handiest of handymen. How do you fix a bannister? It was going to be a GABI job: Get A Bloke In.

We passed an excited Beth on the stairs. So much for her earlier insistence that we both play it cool in front of the agent. 'Just popping up to check out the bedrooms again,' she said with a broad grin. 'Okay to take some pictures?'

'Of course,' said Tim. 'Plenty on our website but knock yourself out.' I wished she'd calm down – her enthusiasm was making me nervous.

We reached the foot of the stairs and the agent ushered me into the kitchen. 'The heart of the house, perfect for your lovely lady and the little one,' he beamed.

'Actually, I do all the cooking,' I said sternly, like it was something I was proud of rather than did under protest. 'Or at least I will do when I stop working. Beth won't have time for it even when she's on maternity leave.'

'Then you'll love this kitchen. Very practical, perfect for a young family, all newly fitted as you can see. So new you can still smell the paint.' He sniffed dramatically to emphasise his point.

I couldn't smell anything and the kitchen looked like it had been lifted wholesale from an uninspiring Ikea display. 'It'll do,' I muttered.

'The appliances haven't even been switched on yet,' said Tim. 'All Bosch. German. The very best you can buy. All included in the price of course.'

'Of course,' I said. 'What's behind that door?' I nodded at a stripped pine door opposite the entrance to the kitchen, its dark knots and untidy filler a stark contrast to the shiny newness of the spotless kitchen.

'Oh, that room? That's the one the seller didn't get time to decorate. Just another room in the basement really.' He grasped the brass door knob and forced the door open. Musty air escaped and assaulted my nostrils.

'Eugh. Needs airing,' I said. 'A bit dingy, too.'

'Basements always are, aren't they? Somewhere to pile the boxes when you first move in maybe? Not the best room in the house but easily remedied with a lick of paint. Would make a good man cave for you.' He tried the light switch but nothing happened. 'Bulb needs replacing, too.'

I poked my head in. It was notably cooler than the rest of the house and the dim light leaking around an old blind in the window wasn't exactly showing the room off at its best. There was a faint smell of bleach, which struck me as odd. There was a staleness to the room as if it had been long unloved and I was glad the rest of the house had at least benefited from redecoration – if it had all been like this room I would have been even more sceptical of the estate agent's wriggling patter.

'Have you seen enough, mate?' asked the agent, closing the door as I stepped back from the room.

'Yes, I think this will do for now. I can always email you if we think of any more questions.'

'Of course.' Tim was already disappearing up the stairs. 'Mrs Collins seems enthusiastic,' he called over his shoulder.

'Buying things we can barely afford has always come naturally to Mrs C,' I said.

Tim's laugh sounded as false as his small talk. His mobile rang and I passed him in the hallway as he answered it with a cringeworthy 'Wassup?'

*

Beth was calling for me again. How on earth were we going to knock the price down if she kept this up? This time she was out in the small front garden. The front door was open and I stepped outside, free of the irritation of my "mate" Tim and his bloody phone.

'Isn't this perfect?' she said.

The front garden I'd only glanced at on the way in. It was like something out of a magazine, an impractical arrangement of impractical white paving slabs and ridiculously large pebbles, an ornamental olive tree potted in a large terracotta urn as the centrepiece. The two council plastic wheelie bins slightly skewed the intended minimalist effect but it would have been churlish to point that out.

'That's a pretty serious fence they've built there,' I said, nodding towards a tall dark wooden screen that must have been eight feet high if it was an inch, separating the garden from that of the neighbouring house, number twenty-six.

Beth scowled. 'Do you have to see fault in everything?'

'I do if we want to get the price down to something more affordable. Didn't you say that this is right at the top end of what we can borrow and the bank was quite adamant they couldn't stretch any further?'

She nodded. 'Which is why this is just so right for us,' she said, dropping her voice to a whisper. 'There's nothing to be done. It's so perfect.'

'I think I saw a damp patch in the spare bedroom and that basement...'

'Ben!'

I shrugged. 'Sorry. You're right.' She always was, and even when she wasn't I felt I was always treading on eggshells and I knew better than to pick an argument, what with the baby due so soon and her being on an emotional rollercoaster most days. It was nice to see her happy for once, not balling her eyes out over the slightest thing. Such levity had become something of a rarity, what with her constant moaning and us being forced to live with her parents while we found somewhere of our own.

'You're right about that though,' she said. 'Maybe replace it with a hedge or something. I wonder why they didn't change it to something less daunting to help sell the house? Doesn't make a good first impression. Looks like they're trying to wall off the neighbours.'

'Don't think I noticed it when we got here, did you?'

She shook her head. 'Where's Tom gone?'

'Tim. I think he's on his phone. Probably telling them that we're ready to make an offer after you raving about the place.'

'Are we?'

'It would be helpful if our friend would actually deign to answer a few of my bloody questions first. And it would be good to see if we can get some movement on that price.'

'But?' Her eyes were hopeful and I suspected her mind was already made up.

'It's a nice front position,' said Tim, emerging from the house having presumably finished his call. 'Very functional. Low maintenance. You'll get olives off that tree in the autumn.'

I doubted that very much. The house was in the east of London, not the south of France. 'What are the neighbours like?' I asked.

The sun ducked behind a lone cloud travelling across the blue sky and Beth pulled her cardigan tighter around her. Oddly, the air had chilled quickly. 'I'm just going to go back in and take a few more pictures,' she said.

'Sure thing,' said Tim, 'but don't take too long. You can always pop back in the week, assuming it hasn't already been snapped up by then.' My heavily pregnant wife attempted to quicken her pace, as if every second suddenly counted.

'The neighbours?' I reminded him.

'Well, I've met the young lady who rents out twenty-two. Or at least she will do – she's still living there herself at the moment, didn't want to try to move tenants in while they had the decorating work here going on. All done now though. She's …' he did an exaggerated glance left and right, '…very attractive. All the guys back in the office like Jane. Works in one of those technology companies so probably minted. That's her BMW over there.' I noted the sports car was almost halfway down the road. I'd been right about the parking.

'And she plans to rent it out?'

'That's her plan. Only long term lets though, looking for professionals rather than students. You'll have no problem with whoever moves in. She's very particular. Our rentals chaps think she's too particular but they're all on best behaviour when she walks in. Like I said, she's quite a…'

'Yeah, I got that. Why doesn't she live there herself?'

'You'd have to ask her. Usually people rent out

because of work commitments, you know, a contract overseas or whatever. I suspect it's something like that.'

'And the other side?'

It was an innocent enough question but the agent's expression appeared to falter for a second and the fixed grin fell from his face. 'I don't know anything about twenty-six I'm afraid. There are no notes on that one. The gardens are a bit of a mess, but I'm sure you could have a quiet word and they'd sort them out. A little unloved, especially the one out the back, that's more weeds than grass, but your seller put up that new fence so you can't really see it from this property anyway. No reports of any kids, if that's what you're worried about.'

'Is it Council?'

'No idea, mate. Probably some old couple who just can't get out to tidy up. You can check online but I wouldn't worry about it if I were you. People move on, you know.'

Beth was back and straight in with the legal practicalities. 'Is this fence at the front their responsibility or ours?' Still too keen though: I noticed the premature "ours" and hoped that the agent hadn't caught it.

'Not sure. You like the house though?'

'Very much,' said Beth.

'Not so keen on the price,' I said quickly. 'Is the seller open to offers?'

Tim looked troubled. 'It's a popular house. We've got another couple interested and…'

'Yes. You said. But you also said it's a buyer's market. You can't have it both ways, can you? And he's looking for a quick sale, you said. And there was that damp I noticed upstairs and that basement room needs some serious attention from a surveyor and…'

'Look, it's Saturday and we close at three, so why don't you and Beth think it over and give us a call on Monday if you want another look before making an offer?'

'I'm not suggesting we're making an offer…'

Tim nodded. 'That couple coming at two have already seen it and this will be their second visit. They were very enthusiastic and…'

'We'll take it!' said Beth. My mouth fell open.

Tim grinned. 'You're offering the asking price?'

'Five thousand less,' I said hurriedly, so quiet I wasn't sure I was heard.

'Okay,' said Tim. 'If you're sure. I'll need confirmation in writing of course. An email will do.'

'I'll do it when we get home,' said Beth, seizing control. It was all too fast for me.

'Excellent,' said Tim. 'Do you need to look inside again, take any more pictures?'

We both shook our heads. 'I think we've seen enough for now,' said Beth.

'I need a drink,' I said quietly.

'I'll go back to the office and sort out the paperwork,' said Tim.

Beth gave me a hug and kissed me on the cheek. I hadn't had one of those for a while. 'Our new home,' she whispered. 'Our dream house. New beginnings.'

I shivered. It had definitely turned colder, but when I looked up there wasn't a cloud in the sky.

II.

The whole move quickly became a bloody nightmare. Hands may have been firmly shaken in May but that was just about the only thing that had gone to plan. The man called Tim proved every bit as shallow and useless as I'd suspected he'd be. He was never in the office when I called and suddenly he appeared to be incapable of answering his mobile. No fear of him bothering to return my calls, either. Cheers, mate.

Our solicitor said that he'd had difficulties contacting the seller, and when he finally did get hold of the elusive bastard he deferred everything to his own solicitor, who then promptly disappeared off the face of the earth. Worse, the last month of Beth's pregnancy coincided with a freak heatwave that made her even more irritable than usual and I was made all-too-aware of her considerable physical discomfort. We bickered and argued like we'd been married forever rather than just a few years. It was grim. Not as grim as what was to follow, but at the time it felt like the end of everything.

But there was no turning back for us. With a pregnancy you can't just give up and call it quits after eight months. And neither of us was brave enough to put the brakes on the house move. "Can't do this" was simply not an option. It didn't matter how often Beth said it.

After what seemed like forever things finally started to move. The seller's phantom solicitor returned at last, albeit with a litany of new questions and requirements that made us both seriously wonder what the hell we had started.

But then everything finally fell into place and signatures were hastily scrawled, contracts were silently exchanged, and Mr and Mrs Benjamin Collins were homeowners.

And by then, of course, we were also parents.

At least that had gone to plan. Sam Collins, all eight pounds seven ounces of his perfect pinkness, arrived at the end of September. We were a family. It was emotional. It was real, the tears and labour had been very real indeed and Beth had sworn like a trooper and called me pretty much every post-watershed insult imaginable as she'd gripped my hand even tighter than the evil Tim in her agony.

But she'd done it, we had done it, and by the autumn we were blessed with both a son and a house for our troubles.

Sam was our everything, and in those first few weeks with him the world and everything else just faded into the background. We were living in a trance and we didn't have the time nor inclination to think about anything else. All that moving shit could wait until later.

Our plan was that Beth would return to work after her maternity leave and I would be at home raising Sam for the first couple of years. I had accepted an offer of redundancy at work to ensure that there was plenty of cash in the bank for the move and, as the mortgage could be covered by Beth's salary alone, we agreed that I was going to stay at home with Sam and do the parent bonding thing, a "house husband" (a phrase we both despised) for a while. I was also confident that I'd be able to pick up the odd scraps of freelance work from the paper I had worked at. I'd been sure to leave on good terms, and the publisher had remained a good friend. It was a plan and I was looking forward to life in our own home with our son. It would be the new beginning we so desperately needed.

But the survey on twenty-four couldn't be ignored. It had been a rude awakening when the large brown envelope had landed with a thud on the mat just days before the contracts were due to be exchanged.

'That's not good,' Beth's father had said, lurking behind me and reading the pages over my shoulder.

'What's not good?'

'That bit about all that damp.'

'All Victorian houses have damp basements,' I said, turning the page over in the hope that the interfering bugger would leave me alone. 'Besides, Beth's checked and the bank say they're happy enough with any work that needs doing as long as we get it completed within two years with warranties. Easily fixed.'

'If you say so,' he harrumphed, implying that he knew better. 'Have you let Arthur have a look at it?' Arthur was his go-to handyman, a builder-cum-plumber-cum-carpenter from the old school. Beth's family worshipped the ground he walked on and hung on his every word.

I never said anything but Arthur made me feel inadequate as a man.

'Not yet,' I muttered.

'You should.'

I sighed and hastily gathered up the surveyor's paperwork and pushed past him out of the kitchen without saying another word.

I couldn't wait to get out of that house. Couldn't bear another minute with my know-it-all father-in-law and Beth's mother who thought all the world's problems could be sorted with a cup of milky PG Tips, two sugars and a slice of Battenberg, a woman living in denial if ever there was one.

'She's a natural,' she had said with a smile despite all the evidence to the contrary. Beth had again locked herself in the bathroom, sobbing dramatically as she left me literally holding the baby outside. Our year of being forced to live in the Granny Flat at her parent's place had felt like one long, painful lesson, and that lesson was that you most definitely don't live with your in-laws. Ever.

As we waited to move out it was obvious to us all that it was going to end in even more tears. And, naturally, it was me who was at fault. One sarcastic comment from Old Father Wisdom too many and I snapped, said a few things I probably shouldn't have and that had been it. Bugger the solicitors, her old man wanted us out. I didn't fight him over that. We needed to escape. Anywhere would do. He gave us a week.

Feeling guilty as the move day approached, I suggested that Beth leave the practicalities of moving house entirely to me.

Looking back, it was a rare example of me actually doing the right thing.

*

The removal men had arrived early on the Thursday. Beth had already packed a few bags for the big day but I had been told to leave all the wrapping and boxing to them. 'For insurance and whatnot,' the woman from Packers had insisted on the phone. Fine, best leave them to it if that's what they wanted. Less for me to do. The removal guys swarmed over our rooms in the basement of Beth's family home like a biblical plague of very conscientious locusts, a blur of tissue paper and bubble wrap moving too fast to follow. In a few hours all of our worldly goods were packed, secured in cardboard for the big day. The mountain of boxes filled every inch of the flat's lounge – how had we managed to accumulate so much stuff in just three years together? The bathroom looked stark and cold with its glass shelves clear of tubes and tubs and toothbrushes, and our tiny kitchenette without pots and pans and plates and jars looked so empty. The rugs had been rolled and stood on end, the curtains taken down, bagged and labelled, the wardrobes emptied onto temporary travelling racks. Only the table, chairs, sofa and our bed remained intact. All I had to do was pack up the bedding, unscrew the frame first thing on moving day morning and that was it. We were ready to go.

'I'm scared,' Beth said as we lay with baby Sam on the double bed, staring at the ceiling for the very last time.

What could I say to that? Too late to change things, far too late. Sam gurgled his happy gurgle.

'Tomorrow,' I said. 'Everything starts again tomorrow.' My voice sounded different, bouncing off the naked walls and the undressed windows. I was excited and anxious at the same time and couldn't imagine my heart ever slowing down. There was no way that I would be falling asleep any time soon. There was just too much to do, so much that could go wrong, too much to think about, too much to...

And I must have gone then, exhausted from the stress and strain of it all, burnt out before it had even really begun.

*

'That's it then?' asked Jerry from Packers. I'd already given him a couple of quid but he was still hanging around, angling for more. I wasn't playing ball and he wasn't man enough to ask.

'Think so,' I said, signing the paperwork with my hurried, clumsy scrawl that looked more like 'Bong' than 'Benjamin Collins'.

'Easiest move we've done in months,' said Jerry. 'Shame we couldn't get the van closer. Parking bit of a bitch around here by the look of things.'

'Yeah,' I said. 'We've only got a Mini though, so

shouldn't be too bad.'

'If you say so, squire. Good luck and everything.' We shook hands and Jerry clambered back into the cab of the van.

I headed back into number twenty-four and closed the front door, *my* front-door, on the outside world.

Home at last.

The hallway was the only place in the entire house with enough space to swing the proverbial cat. Every other room was stacked to the ceiling with tall pillars of cardboard boxes. Maybe me insisting that Beth and Sam stay with her parents until everything was in hadn't been the brightest idea I'd had after all. Maybe telling Jerry and his mate to just put everything wherever and thinking I could easily sort it later hadn't been that smart, either.

Never mind. I'd unpacked a few boxes and even thought I could put up a picture or two to make it feel more like home. Maybe that photo from our wedding day, the professional one in the extravagant frame, where Beth looked beautiful, I looked almost passable and my new in-laws a bit shell-shocked. I'd hang it properly, too, drill a hole and find one of those plastic plug things and a proper screw rather than just tapping in a nail like I normally did. I needed to treat those Victorian walls with a bit of respect.

New beginnings, and all that.

*

'Did you see the state of the toilet?' Beth hadn't been in the house five minutes and I already felt like I was on trial.

'Not me,' I said, for once genuinely innocent.

'Really? Then God knows how long that's been sitting there then. Remind me to get some extra bleach next time we're out.'

'Bad is it?'

'I'm surprised I didn't smell it halfway down the street. Disgusting. Made me feel quite sick.'

I nodded. I honestly hadn't noticed. Been too busy.

'And I see you've managed to put that picture up,' she said. I liked impressing my wife. It didn't happen very often. 'It's not straight,' she added. 'And I think it would look better on the other side of the room, don't you?'

I swallowed hard and nodded. There was no pleasing some people.

*

It was later that first evening and the sun was long gone. The day was lasting forever. Baby Sam was lying in his new cot, eyes open, just staring. He seemed to be fascinated by the new ceiling. Everything was new in his world. It was little things like that I just loved about him.

I hadn't had the time to put together the frame of our own bed yet so we lay on the mattress on the floor.

Beth sighed. We were both shattered.

'Long day. How is it that some days seem to last forever? There's so much to do but I had to get Little Man's bed ready.' Beth nodded slowly and I smiled for the first time in hours. It was nice that she'd noticed a little of the effort I'd put in. I'd been at it non-stop since six that morning. I'd even managed to clear most of the boxes from the lounge and it looked quite presentable in there now. Still no curtains up – that would take a trip to B&Q or three – but at least it was starting to look like a real room rather than a warehouse.

I took her hand and gave it a squeeze.

'We can afford it, can't we? The money's all okay?'

'Probably. Your redundancy cheque's almost all gone though. I just have to keep going.' "Probably?" That wasn't exactly reassuring.

'You think you'll be okay going back to work? It's not that far away now and…'

I stopped. I could see that she needed a hug but I was too tired. We lay in silence.

'You know that Mum said that she's more than happy to get on the train and come over whenever you…'

I shook my head. 'That won't be necessary. I mean, it's great that she's there and all that, but I need to do this on my own. It's my job now.'

She nodded but made no effort to hide the doubt in her eyes. She sighed and turned her back on me.

I lay motionless and stared at the unfamiliar ceiling. Life suddenly felt almost good. Was everything really going to be better now? A car went by and its headlights flashed through the room. 'Need to get those curtains sorted,' I said to myself.

Beth's only response was a snore.

Looking back, I guess that was the last evening I felt we were truly safe at number twenty-four.

III.

'Ben!' Beth was shaking my shoulder. 'Wake up!'

'What?'

'That noise!'

'What time is it?' What was up with her?

'You didn't hear it?'

'Hear what?'

'That crash!'

'What crash?'

'Like something falling down!

'You sure?'

'Glass! It could be a window!'

'You'll wake Sam…'

'He's not asleep – he's just lying there. I'm scared Ben. Go and see what it is.'

'Go and see what what is?'

'There was a crash. Don't pretend you didn't hear it. Downstairs. Like something heavy or someone breaking a window or...'

'I'm not pretending – I was asleep, wasn't I? I didn't hear anything and…'

'BEN!'

'Okay. Okay.' Sam was making baby noises from his cot. I forced myself to sit upright and then crawled over to the edge of the mattress. 'Whereabouts downstairs?'

'In the basement I think,' she said, standing by Sam's cot and lifting him onto her shoulder. 'There, there, little man.'

'Are you sure you can hear noise from down in the basement up here?'

'Yes!'

Really? I wasn't so sure. Two floors down? I ran my fingers through my hair then shook my head in an effort to wake up.

'And Ben?'

'What?'

'Don't do anything stupid.'

It felt like I was already doing something stupid but I was on automatic. 'Don't wait up. Send a search party if I don't return by sunrise.'

I paused by the door and tugged Beth's dressing gown off the hook on the back. I wrapped it around me and pulled the short cord tight. I'm not a big guy by any stretch of the imagination but it was still far too small for me. Must get myself one at some point.

'I don't hear anything down there,' I said. 'Are you absolutely certain? You didn't dream it?'

She sighed, sounding as tired as I felt. 'Of course I'm bloody sure. I haven't been to sleep.' She had, but what the hey.

'Okay, okay,' I mumbled under my breath as I left the bedroom.

*

The landing was still unfamiliar so I turned the lights on before descending. Had she heard something? I certainly hadn't. Nothing at all.

The stairs were narrow and steep, winding down through the three storeys and turning at a small landing between each floor. The carpet underfoot was apparently "too light to be practical" and Beth had already put finding a darker replacement on one of those lists she had already stuck up for me on the fridge door. Replacing the carpet would be one for her LATER? list rather than the more demanding SOON!

or, worse, the no-arguments NOW!! one. We weren't made of money.

I reached the bottom floor and stopped as my hand reached for the basement room's door. What could have fallen? Surely it couldn't have been that one I'd hung yesterday afternoon? I had been meticulous in hanging it – drilled the hole perfectly, taken my sweet time and even found one of those little grey plastic things Arthur would have used and a proper screw, too. No way that could have come down. I pushed open the door and reached around the corner for the light.

What the ..?

I couldn't believe what I was seeing.

Lying in pieces on the floor, its glass shattered, was the wedding picture.

I knelt down beside it. Smashed beyond repair, shards of glass scattered around the broken frame. And the picture itself had been torn in two, and as I picked up the halves I saw that it had somehow ripped almost perfectly down the centre: I had me and my father-in-law in one hand, Beth and her mother in the other.

The wall itself hadn't fared any better. Big chunks

of plaster had broken away revealing exposed bricks, barely any mortar between them. They looked loose enough to remove with bare fingers.

Had I really done such a ham-fisted job of putting that picture up?

Shit. What a mess.

And then I saw something that took my breath away; one of the lower exposed bricks was trembling slightly, slowly wobbling its way out of the wall.

I staggered back into a stack of boxes, almost sending them tumbling.

The brick moved again and then fell loudly onto the floor.

Out of the hole in the wall emerged a rat the size of a small kitten, tumbling down onto the floor then scuttling towards me, its claws clattering on the floorboards.

Before I could think, I instinctively raised my foot and stamped down on it as hard as I could. I felt its bones crunch under my sole and its guts and organs burst through the gritty fur. Warm blood and intestines squirted between my toes, the rodent sticking to the sole of my foot. Still alive, the rat twisted around in panic, attempting to bite me. The sharp teeth were gnashing for my bare ankle so I kicked it away as hard as I could and it skidded across the floor before slamming into the skirting board. It thrashed there for a few seconds, already broken inside but too stupid to realise it was dying, its long tail rapping against the wall, blood pulsing from its broken ribcage.

Its oil-black eyes were staring at me in shock.

I was paralysed, unable to breathe until, after what seemed like an eternity, the rat finally stopped moving. Picking my way through the glass I stepped towards the mangled corpse, the blood on my foot tacky and sticking with each step. The rat twitched, a muscle reflex and I panicked and struggled to suppress a scream.

Man up, buttercup! It was just an overgrown mouse!

I picked up some of the packing paper from one of the boxes and prodded the rat with it. Nothing. Definitely dead. Barely able to look, I scooped the creature and its exposed innards up into the paper. As I held the bundle in my hands I felt it twitch again. That hadn't happened, I thought. It couldn't have. I threw the blood-soaked paper and its contents into one of the empty boxes.

It couldn't still be alive.

Shit. What had just happened? Had a rat managed to force its way through a few loose bricks in the wall, sending the picture crashing to the floor?

Don't fool yourself, Ben. More likely the picture had been too heavy and had brought everything down and the rat had just seen an escape route. I should never have attempted hanging that picture, showing off again, should have left it to Arthur. Now I was going to hear about it again and again and again from Beth.

Brilliant.

I needed to clear the mess away before Beth saw it, or cover it up at least until I could think of a way to fix the wall plaster. I needed to clean my foot as well. Beth would not be happy. I wasn't exactly over the moon myself.

I went into the kitchen and filled the bowl with lukewarm water, squeezing in far too much Fairy. At least I hadn't screamed like a schoolgirl when it had happened. I shuddered then lifted the bowl from the sink and put it on the floor. I plunged my foot into the warm water and cleaned it as best I could.

I dried my foot on a tea towel then lifted the bowl, bubbles sloshing everywhere as I carried it into the basement and made a half-hearted attempt at cleaning away the rat's innards with the wet towel.

Useless.

Giving up, I shunted a couple of heavy boxes over the stain. It could wait. I wouldn't tell her. Not worth the grief. Besides, she was sure to be asleep when I got upstairs.

*

'Well?'

I was wrong. She was still awake. I wouldn't mention the rat.

'It was the picture. Took half the wall with it.'

'I knew it! When will you learn?'

'Don't start.'

'You tidy it all up?'

I nodded sheepishly and she knew I hadn't really. I never did a good enough job with the tidying.

'Arthur can put it up when he comes over.'

Don't say anything Ben, you'll only regret it.

'And you should go around to the neighbours and apologise for waking them in the middle of the night.'

I said nothing for a few minutes while she glared at me.

'I will go next door,' I conceded.

'Good.'

'I can pop round there in the morning.'

'You do that.'

Will that shut you up? I kept the question to myself.

'First thing,' I promised.

'Okay.'

'I doubt they heard anything.'

'I'm sure they did.'

'I didn't,' I said.

She said nothing. I stared into the darkness and then shivered as I remembered that feeling of stamping on a live rat in my bare feet.

'What?' she asked.

'Nothing. Just cold,' I lied. She turned her back on me as if she knew I was hiding something else. 'Nothing at all.'

IV.

There was no way I was going to go back to sleep. I tossed and turned, unable to settle but I couldn't forget that moment: my foot crushing the scampering rat, its skull shattering, the shards of bone piercing the sole of my foot. It had happened in a split second but my mind was having none of that, replaying it over and over again in slow motion, the creature exploding with the impact of my heel as I ground it into the floor. I'd washed the rat's blood, guts and greasy fur from my foot in the bowl as best I could but in bed I could still feel bits of it between my toes and sticking to the sole of my foot.

I gave up on any pretence of falling asleep and got up at six, delicately lifting the covers and making my way out of our bedroom. It was cold, almost icy, and I made a mental note to add 'check the central heating settings' to the fridge's NOW!! list.

The basement room looked even worse in the morning. My attempt at hiding the blood stain under a few boxes was pathetic and I hastily dragged over a few more to improve my chances of getting away with it. If Beth went out later I'd give it a good clean.

The damaged wall though wasn't going to be easy to conceal. I tried stacking a few boxes to make it look better but that was pathetic. Best she saw the damage and I had the lecture. Polyfilla wasn't going to cut it and I'd have to ask Arthur to fix it – plastering was way beyond what I was capable of and I'd just have to grit my teeth when she reminded me how useless I was. I picked up the brick the rat had forced out and slotted it roughly back into the hole.

I heard a loud tut behind me. Beth was standing in the doorway, shaking her head. I had no idea how long she'd been there.

'What a mess.'

I hung my head. No point in arguing. She was right; it was a mess.

She surveyed the damage. 'I said you hadn't put it up properly. Should have let Arthur do it. Can't imagine what you were thinking. How many times before you learn?'

I felt my fingernails biting deep into my palms. At least she hadn't noticed the dark stain on the floor.

'And we need to get these boxes out of here. Packers will want them back or we'll forego the deposit.'

'Yes,' I said feebly.

'Don't forget to go next door and apologise for that noise.'

As if I could.

*

'Hello.'

'Hello?' She was taller than me. Much taller. Maybe even over six foot in her stockinged feet. She was pretty but nothing to write home about. Another lie from estate agent Tim. Not that I was keeping count.

'You must be Jane?'

'I am. Do I know you?'

'I'm Ben. Ben Collins. From next door. Number twenty-four. Me and my wife Beth have just moved in and …'

'Not exactly quiet about it, were you? And that van of yours meant I couldn't even park outside my own house.' There was no smile – she wasn't the smiling type. A pity as she'd be prettier if she could just manage a smile. Maybe she saved those for estate agents.

'Sorry about that. They emptied it as quickly as they could. It's been manic.'

Jane crossed her arms and looked over my shoulder. 'You on your own?'

'My wife's going up to her parents' for the day. I'm best off out of that one. I'm in charge of doing the rest of the unpacking.'

'The removal men weren't exactly quiet. You hear everything through these walls. Paper thin.' Still no smile.

'Sorry.'

'I suppose you want to come in for a cup of coffee?' I couldn't imagine a less enthusiastic invitation.

'That would be nice. Thanks.' The woman turned her back on me, muttering to herself as she walked into the house, leaving me to follow. Maybe this hadn't been such a great idea. I had plenty to do without wasting my time with Miss Frumpy-Grumpy the beanpole.

'It's just like our house,' I said, sounding so pathetic in my feeble attempt to make conversation. 'Only in reverse. You know, like a mirror image.'

'They're all the same, these houses,' she said as we descended the stairs to the basement. 'I'm moving out. Everything's packed already.'

'So I see.' Like ours, her kitchen was on the basement floor, bigger than ours due to a large glass conservatory extension at the back. She already had a dozen or so Packers boxes neatly stacked against the far wall. 'The agent who sold us the house said you were moving out at some point.'

'Have to be out by Friday midday. That bitch of a tenant says she needs to move in earlier than I'd thought I'd agreed and I have to go or the whole deal's off.' She didn't sound happy about it. 'Bloody estate agents.'

'Don't get me started on those shysters,' I joked. She didn't even smile. 'Are you going far?'

'New York. Work.'

'Nice.' The expression on her face suggested it wasn't. 'You go there often?'

'Too often. Hate the fucking place.' She thrust the kettle under the tap and filled it. 'It'll have to be instant. I've packed the Dualit away.'

'That's fine,' I said, trying to sound off-hand but her

coldness was chipping away at my confidence. 'What do you do?'

'Do?'

'For work I mean.' It was like extracting teeth.

'I'm a C.O.O.,' she said, opening a jar of economy label coffee and spooning brown powder into two damp mugs. 'Sugar? I've got no milk.'

'No thanks. Black's fine.'

She didn't wait for the kettle to fully boil and slopped the hot water in, her impatience for me to leave all too obvious.

'What's a C.O.O. do?' I asked. I didn't speak City.

'All the shit,' she said. 'Everyone fucks everything up and I have to wade in and sort it out.'

I offered what I thought was my best sympathetic smile but she didn't return it. 'You haven't packed the kettle yet then? Leaving it until last?'

'Obviously. For the guy from Packers. I figured if I give them enough tea they won't expect a tip.'

'Packers? That's who we used.'

'I know. I had their bloody van outside. They were lucky to find a space. Fucking useless around here. Nowhere to bloody park. Glad I'm going.'

So was I. I took a sip of the coffee. It was, without doubt, the worst I'd ever tasted.

'I don't suppose you heard any loud noises yesterday? Last night? Around two in the morning?'

Her cup paused in mid-air, inches from her lips. She put it back on the table. 'What sort of noises?'

'I put a picture up yesterday, just to make the place feel more like home, but I reckon the old plaster couldn't take the weight and it all came crashing down in the middle of the night. Didn't hear it myself but my wife did and thought it might have woken the neighbours. If you did I'm really sorry and…'

'No, I didn't hear anything.' Her lie was obvious and she seemed to be avoiding eye contact.

'You're certain you didn't…'

'I heard nothing.'

We stood in silence. She wanted me gone. I tried the coffee again. It hadn't improved.

'I'm writing a novel,' I said. It came from nowhere and I immediately regretted saying it. I was rubbish at small talk. 'Well, I will be. Working from home. Had enough of the office life.'

'How fucking delightful for you.' Her casual

swearing unsettled me. Jane walked to the sink and poured the rest of her coffee away.

'I used to work at *The Herald* but I've given that all up now to stay at home and be a good dad, raise our baby Sam.'

She rolled her eyes. 'You've got a baby? Oh, joy.' Her deadpan sarcasm was grating.

'For a few years at least,' I continued. 'Before school starts and everything. My wife Beth's the main earner in the family any way. She works for one of the banks over the river. Big bucks. That's how we could afford the house.'

'He sold it too cheap.'

'Yes. We were very fortunate.'

She laughed. 'If you say so.'

What did that mean? I decided to let it lie and change the subject.

'Did you know the people before us? We never got to meet them and…'

Suddenly she looked alarmed, her pale blue eyes boring into me.

'You don't know?'

'Don't know what?'

'They didn't tell you?'

'Who didn't tell us?'

'The estate agents. They didn't mention it?'

'Mention what?'

She sat down, her face unreadable.

'They didn't tell you about the suicide?'

My mouth dried and I took a gulp from my mug, wincing at the cheap bitterness. I felt my knees weaken and sat down hard on a kitchen chair. 'What suicide?'

'Not surprising. Hardly a selling point. She hacked herself to pieces in the basement.'

'Who did?'

'Sarah. Jack's wife.'

'What, in *our* basement?'

'They didn't even mention it?'

'No.' I felt dizzy, my head spinning, unsure how to react.

'The agents should have told you that. They seemed normal enough neighbours when they moved in. Chatty couple, you couldn't shut her up at times and she was quite funny, too. Claimed she was a bit of a psychic and offered to read my fortune. I thought it was a laugh but I always thought there was something wrong about her. Mind you, it was still a shock when I heard the details. Hacked away at her arms like a butcher, the ambulance guys said. Severed through one of her own wrists. Blood everywhere. Must have been quite a sight. I heard it all. Her screaming and screaming then…' My face must have been a picture. I think I'd stopped breathing.

'Last time I saw her she told me that she'd heard voices talking to her at night and that there were people living in the walls.' She laughed, but whether it was at the memory or my look of alarm I couldn't be sure. 'They should have carted her off to the madhouse straight away after that. Then I would have been spared all that shrieking in the middle of the night and everything. The warning signs were all there. Police and all kinds of nonsense out the front when they came to take what was left of her away.'

'She died?'

She snorted. 'What do you think? Must have been like a fucking abattoir in there.'

'Oh.'

'Not really surprised he moved out after all that and put the place on the market. Must have been pretty hard for him, although he never looked quite right to me either. Don't think I ever saw him again. He couldn't wait to skulk away. Embarrassing.'

'When was this?'

'Not that long ago. Much quieter without them.' She stood again. 'Or at least it was. Didn't you say you were busy?'

I was shaken and wanted to know more but could take the hint. 'I was thinking of going around to twenty-six,' I said, rising to my feet. 'You know, introduce myself to whoever lives there and apologise for the noise last night.'

She sighed. 'Good luck with that one. I bet she won't even open the door. Hardly a bunch of laughs, her.'

'There's a woman living there?'

'Widow, I think. Haven't seen her in, like, forever. Can't even remember what she looks like. Old. Fucking old. Probably older than the house. I wouldn't waste your time. Could even be dead for all I know.' She chuckled but it was cold and humourless.

'Still, I thought it would be…'

'Knock yourself out. What do I care? I'll be gone in

a matter of days.'

And good riddance, I thought.

'You finished with that coffee?'

I hadn't but handed the cup back anyway. 'Thanks for your time and sorry to hear that you're going,' I lied.

She poured what was left of the awful coffee into the sink, then lifted her head and was staring at me again, her eyes wide and intense. 'You should go,' she said. 'Just go.'

I felt my chest tighten and my pulse quicken. No point in arguing with that look. I walked to the foot of the stairs and took them quickly, not looking behind me. She followed me up.

'Nice to meet you,' I muttered on the doorstep, not wanting to look into those eyes again. 'Don't forget to knock and say bye before you go.'

'You should leave,' she called after me as I hurried down the path.

It was only later that I realised that she didn't mean her house.

She meant ours.

V.

When I returned home the atmosphere in our own house was equally chilly.

'I thought you were going to your Mum's?' I said.

'Sam's sleeping,' Beth said. 'And about bloody time, too. Thought I'd best not disturb him after you kept him up all bloody night.'

She was still going on about that. Jesus, woman, give it a rest.

'The woman at twenty-two said she didn't hear anything,' I said.

Beth didn't look up from her magazine.

'The woman at twenty-two. Not a dickie bird.'

Beth sighed and flipped her page.

'Bit snooty. Not the nicest company. Very pretty though,' I said, attempting to provoke a reaction. She looked up and glared at me with such intensity I knew I'd misjudged that one. Couldn't win.

'I guess I'll pop around the other side and apologise to the woman who lives there, too.'

'You do that.'

'Do you want to come with me? Introduce yourself?'

'No.'

'You'll probably be gone by the time I get back?'

'I'd imagine so.'

'I'll just pop next door then,' I said and fled.

*

Life is full of "if only" moments. "If only I hadn't finished that last pint", "If only she'd said yes", and, as I looked up at twenty-six, there was another one: if only I'd paid attention to this particular neighbour when we did the viewing rather than obsessed over the estate agent and haggling over the price. If I'd done that I would have seen what a shit heap the neighbour's place was and run a mile from Amersham Place and then we would have been spared everything that happened on that wretched street.

But I didn't, and life is full of regrets and sliding doors moments like that one.

You couldn't see the property from the street. It was effectively walled off from the outside world; on our side there was that tall fence the previous owner had put up as a screen and at the front on the street was a massive overgrown hedge, growing chaotically in every direction, obstructing the pavement and completely hiding whatever lay behind.

I had to squeeze past it then battle with the rotten wood of a reluctant garden gate before I could finally see the house properly.

The front garden was a tip. It was badly paved, tufts of grass and weeds poking bravely between the broken slabs. A discarded gas cooker stood at a jaunty angle by the bins, its white enamel chipped and flaking, the exposed metal dark with rust.

There was wind-blown rubbish everywhere.

A couple of old black bin liners had been left next to the cooker, ripped open by rats or foxes hunting for scraps of food. I could have sworn I saw something move there.

The house itself looked derelict and unoccupied. The brickwork at some point had been painted red, a very dark red, almost the colour of blood, making it look like something from one of those old fairy tales, the sort parents read to their kids before realising too late they've traumatised them for life. 'It's just a house,'

I muttered to myself. Uncared for? Definitely. Unloved? Almost certainly. But just a house, bricks and mortar. Nothing to be scared of.

Flakes of once-white paint clung to the window and door frames, the grey wood beneath splintered by decades of sun and rain. The front door was a sad faded blue, the paint also cracked and peeling like it was as old as the house itself.

Curtains were drawn across the filthy windows, their linings dark with mould and grime. Not looking where my feet were treading I realised too late that I'd stepped in something soft and felt my stomach sink. Dog shit on the front step. And fresh. Did the woman living there have a dog? She could at least have picked its shit up.

I wiped the sole of my shoe on the step, scraping off the worst of it as best I could.

There was no doorbell. No knocker, either. Not very welcoming but no great surprise either. The house number was an old broken ceramic tile with a large diagonal crack splitting it in two. The concrete surrounding it had crumbled and much of it had fallen.

I knocked on the door, gently at first then harder,

impatient to get this over with.

Nothing.

I counted to twenty. Maybe she was infirm and took a while to get to the door?

I knocked again.

Maybe she was deaf.

'Hello?' I shouted. 'Anyone in?'

Maybe she was dead.

Stop being so stupid, Ben. I knocked again, louder this time. There was still no sign of anything happening behind the curtains or door.

I tried poking open the tarnished bronze letter box with my finger but the stiff spring was reluctant and bit back, catching my finger when it snapped shut.

'I wouldn't bother if I were you,' laughed a voice from the street. By the gate was a postman, clearly amused by my efforts to engage with my new neighbour. He had short blond hair and the ruddy complexion of a man who embraced the outdoor life, his red short-sleeved shirt and cream shorts brightly optimistic on such a cold, dank November morning.

'Is she away?' I asked.

'Don't know about that but no-one's ever answered

when I've tried to deliver anything there.'

'What, never?'

'Not in my time. And I've been doing this round for years.'

'And you've never seen her?'

The postman shook his head. 'Can't remember the last time I had any mail for that place and I don't even bother putting the flyers through now. That letterbox is a killer.'

I smiled, inspecting my sore finger. 'Yeah, I know. Are there foxes around here? I just trod in something distinctly doggie.'

The postman laughed. 'Yeah, you see them some mornings, especially on Mondays.'

'Why Mondays?'

'Bin day. You'll see.'

'I'm Ben, by the way, I'm new at twenty-four.'

'That last guy's in your place's gone, then? Good riddance I say.'

'Why's that?'

'Argumentative bugger. Once had a go at me when something he'd ordered never turned up. Accused me of stealing it. Apparently he went at everyone. Wanker.

Her at twenty-two won't be sorry that he's gone – she hates him.

'She's moving out, too,' I said.

'Not surprised. No-one seems to hang around here for very long. Never seen so many For Sale and Sold boards. Except for her in there, of course.' He nodded at twenty-six.

'You know his wife died?'

'Who, that bloke who sold you your place? That's no excuse for being an arse, is it?'

'Did you know her, the wife?'

He shrugged. 'Seen her at the window once or twice. She rapped on the glass once when I had something to deliver and told me to f-off.'

'I heard it was suicide.'

The postman shrugged. 'That would have been messy. Nothing surprises me around here. No wonder they had to get the decorators in big time. Did she blow her brains out? Nasty. Inconsiderate, too.' He was all heart.

'No, slashed her wrists was what I heard,' I said, scarcely believing the conversation I was having. 'The house looks fine now though. You'd never know…'

The postman laughed. He nodded at twenty-six. 'I reckon that place has a few stories, too. If walls could…'

'Yeah, I know,' I said.

I turned and took one last look up at the house next door. What a dump. I decided to give it one more try and banged hard on the door. 'Hello?' I shouted. Not a murmur. 'HELLO?'

Still nothing. No sign of life.

'Told ya,' chuckled the postman.

VI.

The legend that is Any-chance-of-cash Arthur frowned and tapped the bricks with his knuckles, a man who knew exactly what he was looking at and how to fix it. He took one of his dramatic deep breaths and shook his head. 'That's not good, Bill.' He knew full well that my name was Ben but always called me Bill, a childish joke that seemed to constantly amuse him.

'Not good?' I was braced for bad news – Arthur rarely delivered anything else – but we could have done without the repair costing an arm and leg.

'Those loose bricks,' said Arthur, waving his mug in the direction of the wall. 'Real bit of bodging that. I'll have to completely rebuild that chimney stack most likely, assuming you was thinking of putting the fireplace back in.'

'Oh.' I really wanted to have an open fireplace. That bastard of an estate agent had said that the original one had been bricked up back in the seventies but he had assured me that it would be a piece of piss to re-open it. The survey's finding of damp readings off the scale in the basement were obviously more urgent but I'd hoped for a proper fireplace with crackling logs and wintry smells in the months ahead. Maybe not this winter then. Arthur was rarely wrong.

'Can you fix it?'

'Let me think,' said Arthur, and took a long slurp of his tea, his third already that afternoon. He enjoyed prolonging my agony. And how could one man consume so much tea? 'Do you just want to keep your mortgage people happy or actually want it fixed proper?'

'Depends.'

'Thought so. You can't burn coal or wood here, y' know. Would have to be that smokeless rubbish. Never the same that.' He delighted in giving me bad news. 'Well, it would be messy and time consuming and expensive to rebuild it completely, but I could make it good enough to please whoever they send out to have a look. They won't care as long as they can tick a box and whatnot. No point in doing it properly for 'em. Any chance of a biccie?'

I shook my head. 'Not unpacked them yet.' He looked genuinely gutted.

'Once I repoint the brickwork, bit of re-plastering, slap on some Stain Block and let it dry out. Give it a few coats of emulsion and you'd never know.'

I nodded sagely.

Arthur put his mug down on one of the Packers boxes still awaiting my attention and removed his wireframe glasses, leaning forward to give the broken plaster on the chimney stack wall a closer look.

'That's an odd colour,' he said. 'It looks redder than those other walls, less magnolia, more like, I dunno, pink or somethink.'

He was right. When I looked at it that wall was a different colour. 'Does it matter?' I asked. 'The whole room will need redecorating at some point.'

'What does the Boss reckon? Does she want it pink?' He always referred to Beth as 'the Boss'. His own wife was 'the Management'. Arthur liked his little jokes behind the ladies' backs. God only knew what he said about me behind mine.

'She's not here – she's taken Sam back to our old place. I don't think she's even noticed it. She's not really been in a good mood since we moved,' I said. 'Magnolia's fine by me if you want to make it the same as the other walls.'

'You don't want it done in Farrow & whatsit then? 'Strawberry Hiccup' or 'Elephant's Blush', something like that, those women like that rubbish, don't they?' He gave me a conspiratorial wink and despite myself I nodded. Even before we'd moved Beth had been picking out some expensive new paint colours for the lounge – seven different shades of white that all looked much of a muchness to me. I just went along with it – after all, it was only paint for Christ's sake.

But there was something different about that wall in the basement, and it wasn't just that it was a different colour. It just looked *wrong*. I stood next to Arthur and ran my forefinger across the plaster. It didn't actually feel that damp. I rested my palm on the brickwork – it felt cold, like a window in winter.

'Odd isn't it?' said Arthur and I nodded. 'Feels wet but isn't. Have you spoken to the neighbour on this side?'

I shook my head, sparing him the details of my futile efforts to make contact.

'You know what I reckon? By the look of it, you may be sharing the chimney flue with them. You get that in some of these old Victorian places, so they have two fireplaces either side of the party wall but they meet a few feet up and have just one chimney. I think that's what you've got here.'

'And that's common?' I was never sure if Arthur was pulling my leg or not.

'You see it sometimes.' Arthur took a step back and rubbed the grey stubble that was a permanent fixture on his chin. 'Y'know, now that I come to think about it, I think I did some work along this street a while back.'

'Really?' Arthur always had a story. I heard one once that may even have been true.

'Yeah. Might have even been that place next door. There's always been work going on in this street. Old couple they was, even then. My gaffer thought they was mother and son, but turns out they was married. He was alright but I remember his missus was a complete bitch.'

That was not a phrase he would have used if Beth had been in the room. 'Difficult?'

Arthur laughed. 'Difficult doesn't begin to describe her. Talked all posh like, but would suddenly swear like a trooper. Always telling us exactly how she wanted things done – not like that, like this – and then changing her mind when we'd finished so we had to do it all again. It's like she thought we was just working for her. Miserable so-and-so. Never smiled. Stubborn, too. Once she'd set her mind on something there was no changing it. Never met anyone so … so … what's the word?'

'Tenacious?' I suggested.

'Yeah. Tenacious. That's a good word for her, that. He was odd too, the husband. Never said anything, mind. But then she'd make some sarky comment to him and all hell would break loose. Funny it was. Like we wasn't there. She'd just go at him, F-ing and blinding like a navvy. That bitch was difficult, alright.' He chuckled. 'Haven't thought about them in years.'

'Surely she can't be the same woman living there now?' I muttered to myself.

Arthur shrugged. 'What's she look like?'

'I haven't seen her yet.' I had been back next door three times and there was still no answer.

'If it is her she must be ancient by now. Wouldn't be surprised if she topped him herself. Always thought one of 'em might snap and lose it when they had one of their ding dongs.'

I couldn't tell if he was joking or not. I never could with Arthur.

'I tell you another thing,' he was in full flow now, 'they had a bloody great dog, too. Massive black Labrador. Vicious bugger. Nearly took old Tom's hand off when he tried to pet it.' Arthur chuckled at the memory. 'Never seen a monster like it. Snapped at air like he was trying to bite it in half. Nasty piece of work. Nobody liked that beast.'

Arthur did like to talk. If I couldn't get him out soon he'd be expecting another cup of tea and I was low on milk as it was.

'So you can fix it?' I asked, eager to get back on topic and Arthur away before Beth returned.

'Yeah, I should think so.'

'When could you start?'

'I've got quite a bit on at the moment but can probably do next week.'

'And will it be ..?'

He shook his head. 'Couple of hundred. Take all that off,' he waved his empty mug at the wall, 'make good, lick of magnolia. Couple of days at most.'

I breathed a sigh of relief. That was quite affordable. 'And while you're here,' I said, pushing the boxes a few feet to the left to uncover the spot where I'd had my big rat moment. 'Any idea how I get rid of a stain like this?'

'What is it? Red wine or summat?'

'No idea. Looks old.'

Arthur crouched down for a closer look. 'Yeah. I reckon that's a wine stain. Could have been there a while. That'll be a bugger to remove. You got a sander?'

I shook my head. I didn't even have sandpaper.

'I tell you what I'd do. Cover it up. Get a big rug and just cover it.'

I nodded. I knew Beth would buy that if it was Arthur's recommendation.

Arthur was inspecting the bottom of his cup with a hopeful eye. 'Any chance…'

'I'll take that for you. So, you can start on Monday?' I started to usher Arthur back up the stairs and towards the front door.

'Tuesday probably,' said Arthur, twisting the knob

on the door. 'Anything else you want me to have a look at?'

'Beth will have a whole list for you by then I'm sure,' I said. 'See you Tuesday at nine then.'

'Nearer ten. What's the parking like around here then, Bill?'

I just smiled and quietly close the door behind him.

*

I was quietly pleased with myself. Much to my own surprise I had managed to put together two entire Ikea bookcases without assistance from Arthur. And, as there was no point in re-hanging the wedding picture until the work on the wall was finished, I was all done. Might even pour myself a wee whisky and…

I heard the key in the front door.

Maybe not.

Beth stomped down the stairs. She put Sam's rocker on the kitchen floor and went to the sink to wash her hands.

She had a face like thunder.

'What's up? I asked

'Don't ask.'

'Anything I can help with?'

She scowled.

'How's Little Man been?' I asked, unbuckling Sam from his car-seat-cum-rocker and lifting him out. He smiled and my heart skipped.

She sighed. 'Fine. Did Arthur come 'round?'

'Yep. All sorted.'

'Okay.' Not "thank you", just "okay". 'When?'

'Starting next week. Couple of days' work he reckons. Not all good news though. There's a nasty stain on the floorboards in the basement he spotted. Red wine he said. Soaked right into the wood. Needs some serious sanding action he reckons and…'

'Can't be that bad, surely. We've got that old rug from Mum's house we can use to cover it.' Something in her tone suggested she wasn't really listening.

We said nothing for a few minutes while she made herself a cup of tea, not offering me one. I suspected she'd had a row with her mother but it turned out I was wrong.

'Ben?'

'What?' It was never good when she used my name.

'Work called. I've got to go in next week. They want me back early.'

'But…'

Mug in hand she was already halfway up the stairs. 'Nothing I could say to change it,' she called over her shoulder. 'Big meeting. They need me there.'

'Don't you want to have a look at the shelves and help with the last of the boxes?' I called up after her but she was already out of earshot.

Back to work already? She'd only been off work a couple of months and was entitled to at least one more.

But I was starting to think the new house would be a happier place without her. Everything was an argument and I couldn't get anything, not a single damn thing right. She'd been in a bad mood from day one and I hadn't even told her half the stuff I'd found out. Was it Post Natal thingummy? I had no idea. It had started in the summer and every day seemed to get worse and worse.

It was like she couldn't bear to stay in there with me a second longer than she absolutely had to. Maybe she'd feel differently once she got back to her office desk and the real world of banking, rather than the slightly unreal life we were living at home.

Maybe, but I doubted it.

VII.

'I had a little accident,' I said. I was angry with myself, angry with the world.

'What?' Her eyes blazed at me. 'Is the Mini okay?'

Not "what happened?" or "are you okay?". No, she had other priorities, confirming what I'd always suspected; she loved that car more than me. Mind you, that wasn't actually saying much.

'Just a dink on the boot door. It wasn't easy squeezing it into the only space free down the road. Those bloody skips just sit there for weeks and..."

'How big a dink?'

I pinched my fingers to show a gap of just a few millimetres. 'Tiny. You wouldn't even notice if I hadn't mentioned it.'

Her look suggested she thought otherwise.

'It'll pass the MOT, if that's what you're worried about. Anyway, I got those curtain poles. They're extendable. Brushed chrome and…'

'You can put them up while I'm at the doctors for Sam's check-up.' She glanced at her watch and scowled, grabbing her bag and lifting Sam in his rocker into the crook her arm. She was late for the appointment. That was my fault too. 'You think you can manage that on your own? And can you get those spare keys cut today?'

'And unpack those boxes you were going on about last night?'

'Yes. And before I forget,' she said, poking in her bag for something, 'Have a look at the baby monitor, will you? I kept hearing a radio station on it. Sounded like a play. Must be some kind of interference thing. Probably just needs a tweak.'

It was a baby monitor, not Jodrell Bank. I doubted very much there'd be anything to tweak. 'I'll have a look,' I said. Was it me or were her demands non-stop?

'And I've added more stuff to the list on the fridge.'

I grimaced. 'That list must be a mile long by now … does it still fit on the fridge?' It was meant as a joke. Her face told me my sarcasm wasn't in the least bit appreciated. 'Will you be long?' I asked.

'I'm late thanks to you,' she said, wearily shifting Sam's rocker to her other arm. 'I called to let them know but they say I might have to wait for the doctor.

Thanks for that.'

I knew better than to protest my innocence. 'The car's right down the road,' I said. 'Near the corner. You might have trouble getting it out and…'

'Jesus, Ben, you're all great news today, aren't you?'

And with that, she was gone, the door slamming behind her.

The silence that followed was heaven.

*

Putting up a couple of curtain poles should have been a doddle, but me, a step ladder and a power tool was never going to be a winning combination and it took four attempts at drilling the holes and the best part of an hour until I had the poles in place.

They didn't look straight. Mind you, nothing in the house looked right. I'd had to choose between making the poles straight by my spirit level or parallel to the wonky ceiling and coving. Not thinking, I had opted for the latter and now the curtains had a life of their own, sliding effortlessly down the pole with minds of their own rather than staying put like they should.

'Never mind, she'll never notice. You've done well there, mate. Job done.' Even I wasn't convinced.

There was still no sign of Sam and Beth coming back so I went upstairs to unpack a few more boxes, a job so simple even I wouldn't be able to bollocks it up.

The tiniest room in the house was to be Sam's. It was next to ours at the top of the house and would be big enough at least until he started school. I'd already suggested that we'd have to look at a different arrangement then but it seemed so far, far away. I had originally thought that the basement might be a possibility but that was never going to happen now that I'd learned that it was Suicide Central down there. After what I'd learned of that room it was not somewhere I wanted to use for anything – best lock that door and throw away the key.

We didn't have much to put into Sam's room. Some clothes and toys we'd received as presents; a small pile of tiny onesies that were too big for him; some little booties and two pale blue cardigans Beth's mum had crocheted for him out of the cheapest looking wool imaginable. Ghastly things – my skin itched just looking at them. When we'd unwrapped them in the hospital I'd suggested that the arms looked too long for a baby and were more suited to the alien from Close Encounters.

Maybe I shouldn't have said that aloud.

I unpacked the box, lining up the little piles of clothes and other well-intended gifts, as well as a few of our own premature purchases, on the room's window sill.

There was just one other box in the room to unpack. It was a plain brown box, no Packers logo and, for once, sealed with very little packing tape. I had no idea what it contained. On the top it just said "Sam" in a messy handwriting that looked like neither mine or Beth's. I didn't think anything of it – maybe it was one of the guys from Packers who had written on it.

I tore open the lid. It was overflowing with bubble wrap, its contents hidden. I plunged my hand in and caught it on something sharp. Surprised, I pulled my hand sharply out and saw that my forefinger had a deep cut, the blood quickly surfacing. Sucking my finger I lifted out the top layer of plastic wrap to find a long, serrated bread knife.

What was that doing in this box? It wasn't even our

bread knife, and why was it not wrapped properly?

I swore and sucked the blood from my finger again. That could have been nasty. I'd be having words with those Packers people. At least it wasn't bleeding too badly.

Underneath the stupid knife, loosely wrapped in stiff tissue paper, was a large book. I lifted it out of the box and unwrapped it.

Bloody hell, talk about a blast from the past. It was a photo album, probably the only actual photo album Beth and I owned.

It was of our wedding. Much happier times.

I sat on the floor cross legged and started turning the pages slowly.

There were my Mum and Dad, captured one last time on film just weeks before the car accident that stole them both away. It was supposed to be a joyful day, the wedding of their only child, but in the picture they looked more confused than happy, as if they'd just discovered that their time was almost over. Mum was staring beyond the photographer's lens seeking something in the distance. Dad was just looking at her, lost in thought.

God, I missed them. They never got to meet my boy. I blinked hard, sniffed and wiped my nose on my shirt sleeve.

I turned the page and there were Beth and I. It had only been taken a few years ago but we looked years younger in the pictures. Beth's hair was longer, straighter, beautiful, her afternoon at that extortionate Charles Worthington salon worth every penny. I think her dress was from Nicole Farhi or one of those other overpriced places in Covent Garden. She had never looked more beautiful and I thought I was the luckiest man alive to have married her. You could see it in my face.

Where did that feeling go?

And me? I looked uncomfortable in my cream linen suit. Actually, it was my only suit. Bought from Next for an interview for a job I never got (never wanted it anyway) and had been gathering dust ever since. I'd been more aware of the discount on the price tag than the style of the jacket or length of the trousers. Even for linen it looked untidy and I hadn't bothered getting it cleaned or pressed for our big day. My can't-believe-my-luck grin in the photo made me look like an idiot.

No wonder her family and friends said at the time she could have done so much better. I'm sure it's said a lot at weddings, but not directly to the groom himself.

Looking back though, maybe I hadn't been so lucky that day after all.

Another page and a picture of all the wedding guests together, both family and friends and…

Enough! What was I doing? I knew this would happen, I'd lose myself in something and before I knew it the afternoon would be over and I'd have done little to diminish Beth's never-ending list of urgent things that only Ben can do.

I put the photo album on the floor and returned my attention to the box. I thought that this was supposed to be full of Sam's stuff? And hadn't we lost that album anyway, when we'd been kicked out of the flat and had to move in with her parents'?

I pulled out more bubble wrap and found another photo album. This one was unfamiliar, with a scratched blue plastic cover I couldn't recall seeing before. Confused, I lifted it out and sat down on the floor again, resting the book on my crossed legs.

These were not photographs of us. At first I thought

they might be of a couple from Beth's side of the family. They weren't her parents but maybe some cousin or uncle or someone. The groom, a balding man with a dark goatee and frameless glasses, was smiling uncomfortably at the camera. By contrast, his bride was younger, not quite pretty, with a manic grin and her eyes suggesting she was high on life or something more chemically-based. They were an odd couple, casually dressed for a wedding. His jeans wouldn't have looked out of place on an old episode of Top Gear, her dress looking distinctly charity shop.

I had no idea who these people were.

I flipped the pages. Photos of family, I supposed, and other guests. Then I froze.

A picture of the house. *Our* house. Twenty-four Amersham Place. With that couple, still in their wedding clothes, standing proudly outside it. The brickwork was darker, the wood of the windows and door looked less pristine but it was definitely the exterior of the house we now lived in.

Who were these people and why were they outside our house?

And what were these photos doing in that box

marked "Sam"?

Fascinated, I turned the page. Another full-page photo, this one indoors was of the woman again but, judging from her appearance, taken a little later. She was holding a very young baby, possibly even younger than Sam, but the woman didn't look happy and her smile was forced. The photograph was dark, as if the flash had failed, and it had a melancholy quality that made me keen to turn the page.

The next picture was of the woman again, alone this time in a field on a hot summer's day. I wondered where the baby had gone. Her eyes suggested a sadness that made me hold my breath.

I was intruding. Intruding on someone else's life. I had to stop. I stood but was reluctant to put the book down.

One more, just one more picture.

I turned the page and…

I dropped the book on the floor, reeling in horror at the photo of a bloodstained room and a butchered corpse staring at me from its pages. It was like one of those police photographs of a massacre. The bloody face, with its gazing yet lifeless eyes, looked like the woman from the other photos.

I recognised that window. The room was our basement and the knife in the pool of blood was the breadknife I had just cut myself on. It took all my self-control not to scream.

Was this the woman who killed herself in our house? Confused, I rose from the floor and kicked the book away, steadying myself by resting my hand on the rim of the box, dizzy in my confusion. What else was in there? I tore away at the bubble wrap and found at the bottom some small packages, all loosely wrapped in stiff off-white paper. I lifted one out. It was light, scarcely more than the weight of the paper itself. I unwrapped it.

It was an arm. A baby doll's arm. What the hell was that doing in a box that was supposed to be full of Sam's stuff?

The arm was rubber, but the hand was lifelike, the finger nails unnervingly like Sam's own. I turned it in my hands quite unsure what to make of it. Three more parcels were a similar size and shape. The doll's other limbs, I wondered? Why had someone dismembered a doll and packaged it with photo albums, one of which

I'd never seen before and never wanted to see again?

Two more parcels remained. They were bigger and squatter and one, the larger of the two, was the size of a small melon. I picked it up and lifted it out of the box. It was heavy, much heavier than the others. Whatever was inside felt hard and solid. The paper was more tightly wrapped on this one and I rolled it in my hands as the paper fell away.

It was the head of the doll. But, unlike the arm and presumably the rest of the body, it was made of china rather than rubber, as bald as a real baby's head and …

I turned its face towards me and my jaw dropped in horror, the doll's head falling from my hands and smashing into pieces as it struck the floor.

It had Sam's face. There was no mistaking it, the dismembered doll in the box had my son's face.

*

It couldn't have been Sam's face. Couldn't possibly be his face. And why on Earth was there a dismembered baby doll wrapped in paper in our boxes? And what was that strangers' photo album all about?

It was almost as if something was trying to scare us away.

I couldn't tell Beth. What could I say that wouldn't make her think I was losing my mind?

It didn't matter – she wasn't listening to me half the time anyway. She was still at the doctor's and besides I'd never been man enough to take her on when she was in one of her moods.

I'd found the dustpan and brush and cleared away the fragments of china, no longer the likeness of my son, just shards of white and pink porcelain. I tipped them back into the box and threw in the photo album of strangers. They weren't ours. Packers could take that all back when they called to collect the empties – I never wanted to see any of that stuff again.

And I needed a drink.

VIII.

'Ben?'

I put my glass down, my cheeks flushing. It was only a small whisky but that didn't stop the guilt.

'Sorry,' I said quietly.

'That was work on the phone.'

'Again?'

'It was the pre-meet prep.' Sometimes she spoke a completely different language. 'They pretty much told me today that the entire department will need to look for new jobs next year.'

I felt the floor tilt beneath my feet and had to sit down. 'Please tell me you're not serious?'

'All the back-end stuff, the finance and HR and IT departments, that's all going to be centralised somewhere not here. All the strategy and management's going to come from corporate in New York. Nothing for me I reckon.'

'No ...'

'Yes. It'll be a disaster, everyone knows it will be a mess and those lucky enough to hang on to their jobs next year won't feel lucky for long. It's not going to be worth me trying to hang on.'

I shook my head. 'But we need that job. We can't afford this house without it.'

Beth was staring at me. 'Maybe that's not such a bad thing,' she said.

'What do you mean?'

'Are you happy here, Ben? Are you really happy?'

I attempted a smile but she wasn't fooled one bit.

'Really? You don't seem it. Or are you just relieved to get away from Mum and Dad's?'

I took another sip from my glass. 'Well yes, there's an element of that, but it's still early days. We've got to make it our home, for us and Sam. You can't expect all the change we've been through to be easy – it will take work, it will take some time. We'll get there in the end, I promise.'

'Not if I haven't got a job, we won't.'

That was true but I really couldn't process what she was saying. 'They won't let you go. Why would they have promoted you last year if they weren't planning on keeping you?'

'Maybe they were buying me for another twelve

months to work through the transition?'

'That's very cynical.'

'It's a cynical world. This is how it works now. I just need to find something new. We've got a little of your redundancy to keep us afloat while I have to look.'

'Maybe I should look too?'

She didn't say anything but her scepticism was obvious.

'You realise Sam hasn't slept properly since we moved in? I know it's only been a few nights but I think he likes it here even less than I do.'

I couldn't believe what she was saying. 'You really don't like it here, do you?'

She stared at me. 'No, I don't. And it's changing us, too. You've been horrible since we moved in.'

'I haven't!' My denial was too loud, amplified by the whisky.

'You have. Surly and sarcastic. Everything's too much bother. I don't know what's up with you.'

And I don't know what the fuck's up with you, I said in my head. 'You were the one…'

She shrugged. 'That was forever ago. This is now. I'm not happy here.'

Looking back, I should have seen it coming, but it was a shock. 'I had no idea you felt so strongly about…'

'Maybe I'm being too emotional, what with work and Sam and everything, but I know that this … this house doesn't feel good, doesn't feel right. There's a sadness and a real anger in these walls. I know you feel it, too. It's not a happy place. I get the feeling it's never been a happy place.'

I swallowed hard. She didn't know the half of it. What she said was cutting me to the core, but…

…but deep down, deep, deep down, I understood. She was right. This wasn't a nice house, a happy home, and never had been. It was an angry house. It didn't want us there. It wasn't evil but there was something eerie, off-key, sinister, when the front door closed and the skies darkened outside. I took another sip of my drink and found it suddenly tasted sour on my tongue. I shuddered as I swallowed it.

'That's all there is to it,' said Beth, so quietly I almost missed it.

I couldn't look at her and stared at my lap. 'S'okay,' I said, blinking something from my eye.

IX.

It was dark outside. I was beginning to dread the dark.

We were lying on our bed, Sam gurgling and squirming between us. The experts all said that sharing your bed with a new-born was the worst way to indulge a child but Beth was right: Sam wasn't sleeping and we were getting desperate. In his cot he lay motionless, wide-eyed, coo-ing or grizzling the night away. But when we put him in our bed his eyelids grew heavy and he was at least quiet.

We were both terrified that we might crush him in our sleep so we lay stiffly in our cold bed, the duvet loose so as not to smother Little Man.

'Those curtain rails look wrong,' she said.

I said nothing.

'And there are still boxes that need doing.' Her needle was hitting a too-familiar groove.

'There aren't that many boxes left. Maybe half a dozen at most.'

'We have to get this place in shape before I go back to work.'

'I know.'

'Look, if you can't be arsed why don't you take Sam over to Mum's tomorrow and I'll empty them?'

I couldn't face her parents again so soon. My silence spoke volumes. My mind was full of expletives.

'Fine,' she said, making it clear that it wasn't. 'Then I will take him over there. Get some fucking perspective for Christ's sake. Thanks for your help with everything, Ben.'

You're welcome. Bitch.

*

I was woken at ridiculous o'clock by a dog barking.

I'd been dozing, sort of on duty, half listening out in case Sam started grizzling. But Sam was quiet even though his eyes were wide, his delicate breathing barely audible as he lay between us.

That dog, however...

It must have belonged to one of the neighbours. I hadn't noticed any dogs barking before, not at night anyway, and the only dog I'd noticed when pushing Sam around the streets trying to get him to sleep had been a tiny Norfolk Terrier who didn't look as if he could muster enough might for a yap, let alone a noise like this. The terrier's name was Ralph. It's funny what people call dogs these days – you don't see too many puppies called "Fido" or "Butch" around.

This one though sounded vicious, like a police dog or some other massive monster of a hound. Maybe it was warning off an intruder? It didn't sound at all friendly. It was snarling viciously and I could picture razor-sharp fangs dripping saliva, its jaws snapping at the air. And it didn't sound like anyone was trying to control it or calm the beast down.

'Wazatnoize?' mumbled Beth.

'It's a dog.'

'A dog?'

'Yes. And a bloody big one by the sound of it.'

'Sounds like it's downstairs,' she said, her voice still heavy with sleep.

'It's not downstairs. How can it be downstairs?'

'Go back to sleep. It can't bark all night.'

I wasn't so sure about that, and going to sleep was easier said than done as I felt wide awake. The dog had now added wolf-like howling to its barking and growling repertoire. 'Jesus,' I sighed.

'Has it been doing that for long?'

'Woke me about five minutes ago.'

'It sounds in pain, don't you think?'

'It sounds angry, like it's taking on a burglar.'

She pulled herself up on her elbows, half-awake but concentrating hard. 'Listen ... you hear that whine just then? Maybe it's hurt.'

'Good.'

'Jesus Christ, Ben!'

'The owner should be taking it to a vet if there's something wrong, not keeping the whole bloody street awake.'

'You're all heart.'

'Shall I call the police?'

'The police?'

'It's disturbing the peace.'

She glanced over at her alarm clock. 'Shit. It's not even three yet.'

'You don't think it's next-door, do you? There was some shit in the garden when I tried calling around ...'

Beth turned her bedside light on. 'I can't go back to sleep if it keeps this up.'

'Have we got any cotton wool?'

'Don't think you've unpacked it yet.'

'Must be one of those boxes without a label and … WILL YOU SHUT THE FUCK UP?!!!' I shouted at the top of my voice.

Beth sighed. 'Well, that'll help a lot.' She looked over at Sam. His little legs were squirming but at least his eyes were now closed. 'There, there, Little Man,' she said, soothingly. 'Daddy didn't mean it. He likes doggies really.'

'No I bloody don't.'

'If it worries you that much, put a coat on and go around there. It definitely sounds like it's coming from next door to me.'

'I'll go and try her again first thing in the morning.'

'Fantastic.' Beth lay down again and curled up into her familiar foetal position, her back turned to me.

'Or maybe I should do it now and get up and go around to the neighbour I've never seen and demand that her dog's put down in the middle of the night?'

Beth said nothing.

Suddenly the barking stopped. The silence was deafening, too good to be true.

'Maybe it heard me,' I said.

'Aren't you the fucking hero,' muttered Beth and my fists clenched under the duvet.

X.

I slammed our front door shut, cursing under my breath.

'What did she say?' Beth called from downstairs.

'Still not bloody answering. Could be dead in there for all I know. Maybe that was why the dog was barking…'

No reply. I headed down the stairs. The two of us being so tired and irritable was a recipe for fireworks, just needed something said out of turn and off they'd go. Add in the stress of Beth getting ready to go into work for that meeting and you'd probably see the resulting explosion from the moon. I needed to calm down – things were tense enough as it was.

She was in the kitchen, Sam was on her lap, one last feed before she left for her bloody meeting.

'Still no sign of life behind those curtains. If someone actually is in there, she's bloody rude.'

'Maybe she's embarrassed.'

'The postman said he'd never heard any dog barking next door and they always bark at postmen, don't they?'

'If you say so,' muttered Beth, removing Sam's lips from her nipple, a gentle pop coming from his mouth.

Why did it always feel as though everything was just a few words away from an argument?

'All fed?'

She sighed. 'Hopefully he'll sleep while I'm out.'

'You'd better go. Hand him here and I'll put him down upstairs.'

I took the slumbering Sam in my hands, marvelling again at just how light he was and settling him over my shoulder.

'Don't forget to check the baby monitor,' she said.

'I won't.'

'And don't bother with putting up that picture. Arthur can do it next week when he's here.'

'Of course.'

Beth sighed. Everything I said to her seemed to be answered with a sigh. Whatever happened to those little smiles of hers? It wasn't me, it was definitely her.

'I'll set the telly up today,' I said. 'I think there's an aerial so I'll see if I can get it to work. Or I could get Sky in to …'

'How many times? I'm not having a dish on the house. You could get the internet and the phone working though – that would be something.'

Easier said than done. I didn't fancy spending the entire day on hold to some Indian call centre trying to get our ancient technology working. Couldn't she just use her bloody mobile?

'Okay. And if I hear a dog again I'll pop round and shoot it, I promise.'

'That would be great,' she said, not listening. She hoisted her bag over her shoulder and kissed Sam gently on the top of his head.

'You have a good morning,' I said, following her up the stairs.

'I won't, she said. 'Call me if you need me.'

'I won't.'

*

The baby monitor crackled into life, making me jump. To be truthful I'd forgotten all about it, had pretty much even forgotten I had a son to look after as I had been so confused by the baffling jargon of the computer's instruction manual. At least I'd managed to get Sam's monitor working without taking a Masters in advanced electronics. He sounded happy enough to me and I couldn't help but smile listening to his cooing on the tiny speaker. I pictured those little legs and arms waving, his tiny fingers clenching and opening as if trying to grasp his new world.

If only everything in life was so simple as …

'You must go,' growled a deep voice, almost lost in the monitor's static. 'You are not wanted here.'

What the ..?

I dropped the manual and froze.

I couldn't tell if it was a man or woman. My mouth dried and my throat tightened.

Who said that? Who the fuck was that?'

'Leave,' it said, and then a throaty smoker's laugh and I heard Sam chortle in response. 'You are not wanted here.'

'Sam!' I shouted as panic gripped me and I bounded up the stairs, two, three at a time. My ankle twisted painfully on the landing and I almost fell, having to desperately grasp at the unsteady bannister to balance myself.

'Sam!' I yelled again. Breathless, I reached the top of the stairs and ran into our bedroom.

The cot was by the bed.

Sam was in the cot.

There was no-one else in the room.

Sam was staring into space, a single blanket draped loosely over him just as I'd left him an hour ago.

I sat on the bed, gasping for air after the sudden exertion, the strength gone from my legs, my hands shaking, my heart pounding.

The baby monitor's speaker crackled as if it was laughing at me. But of course it wasn't. It was a simple baby monitor, an inanimate object.

The thought of taking a hammer to it crossed my mind. Stop it, I scolded myself. Don't be so pathetic. It was probably a crossed signal from a neighbour's monitor cutting into our own. I picked the monitor up and flipped it over. There was a small switch for two channel settings on the side. It was set to "I". I changed it to "II" and put it back next to Sam's cot. Simple. I leant over and kissed his forehead. 'Don't tell her,' I whispered. 'Let's just keep this between you and me.'

I left him in our bedroom and went back down to

the basement. I flipped the switch on the second monitor to "II" and held it to my ear. I could hear Sam's gentle breathing. I smiled. You can be such a fucking idiot at times, Ben Collins. Bet it happens to new parents all the time. If Beth was ever in a half-decent mood again I'd tell her and we'd laugh and laugh, oh how we would laugh.

I needed a drink. I'd put some Peroni in the fridge the night before. It was early, too early, but what the hey?

And as I sauntered into the kitchen I heard the monitor crackle again and that same, unnatural voice whispered,

'Go!'

I froze then shook my head.

Just my imagination, surely. A radio station, like Beth had said.

What else could it be?

XI.

We were eating pizza.

Again.

I never really liked pizza and takeaway pizza is the very worst. Always cold, always dry and tasteless. Always expensive. The kid on the bike had scowled at the pound tip I had rewarded him with. What did he expect? He'd taken almost an hour to deliver two cardboard boxes that were probably more nutritious than their contents.

I hadn't told Beth about the voice on the baby monitor. I hadn't mentioned the rat or finding the doll or the photo albums either. I was storing away too many secrets. Not really lying as such, more a considerate withholding of information, a reluctance to say anything that might tip us both over the edge. Fragile didn't begin to describe her mood and the last thing I was going to do was stoke that fire. Not intentionally, anyway.

I chewed in silence, the dry dough tumbling in my mouth like laundry. 'This is inedible,' I managed to say between unswallowable mouthfuls.

Beth just shrugged. I didn't know if I preferred her stormy silences or the snappy sarcasm.

We had opened a bottle of Rioja but my half-filled glass was untouched. Beth was already on her second. Miracle of miracles, Sam was actually asleep.

Beth picked at the rubbery mozzarella on her slice in silence. She looked close to tears. I was eating too fast, taking greedy bites to avoid conversation and then struggling to swallow them. Beth picked up her glass and took a large gulp of the red.

'We need to talk,' she said.

'I don't feel like talking.'

'I'm not happy, Ben,' she said, ignoring me completely.

I nodded. 'You said.'

'I thought Sam would make things different between us.'

'Give him a chance – he's barely been with us five minutes!'

Her eyes were filling with tears. 'I'd hoped this house would change things.'

'We've not even been here a week.' My voice

sounded brittle. 'We've got to give it time and…'

'I hate this house.'

'But…'

'When you went out today and left me on my own, I felt so alone, so isolated, and when that dog started barking again this afternoon and woke Sam, I couldn't stop crying. I felt so bloody useless.'

'You should have called me.'

'And what? What exactly? Have you belittle me? Tell me not to be so ridiculous, that it is all in my head? That it's early days?' I just stared at her. 'How long do I give it Ben? Weeks? Months? Years? Sometimes you just know, sometimes you can tell something isn't going to work no matter what we try. That's how I feel. My life feels,' she paused, searching for the word, '…broken.'

'I'm sorry.'

'And stop saying you're sorry. Please stop that.'

'Sorry.'

Hilarious, Ben.

'Don't be so fucking childish. I'm serious. I realise that it sounds ridiculous after just a few days but I think I need a break from here, it's making me constantly on edge. If I'm going to stand a chance of keeping that job when I go back to work my panic attacks have to stop. I need to get away from this place and from …'

'Me.' I finished her sentence for her.

'Yes.'

Something inside me broke.

She continued: 'Not forever, at least I hope not, just for a week or two. Get my head straight'

'But when we first came here you loved this house and…'

'Yes. It feels like I was a completely different person then. I don't love it now. I hate it. I really, really hate it. I feel like it's going to kill us, Ben.'

I reached across the table to take her hand but she pulled away. She couldn't meet my eyes. I felt I'd left it too late to tell her what I'd learned about the house – if I mentioned that she'd bite my head off.

'What do you want to do?' I asked.

'I'm thinking of staying at Mum's,' she said. I'd feared she'd say that. 'Mum can look after Sam when I'm working.'

'I can't go back there yet.'

'Without you.'

That one stung but I bit my tongue.

'I'm hoping that just being away from here, from you, just for a short while, will be enough.'

I felt numb. 'One more week please,' I said. She shook her head.

'I can't continue like this,' she said through the tears. 'I'm sorry.'

I knew it wasn't working but that didn't make it easy to agree with her. Okay, the tension between us was unbearable at times but I didn't have a clue how to even start fixing it.

And, ridiculous as it sounded, that bloody house was breaking us up.

'It's the house and …'

'It's us. Can't you see that?'

I shook my head. 'No, it's this house and its ghosts and…'

'That! Stop right there. That bullshit about this place. It's US!'

'But … but don't leave me. Not tonight.' I said it so quietly I wasn't sure she'd heard me.

'Tomorrow.'

She had.

She drained her glass and lifted Sam from his chair, taking him up the stairs without a word.

It took all my strength not to cry. Or shout, rage and tell her what I really thought.

But I said nothing.

XII.

I was still drinking. I had brought the rest of the Rioja bottle up to the bedroom with me and it was now empty.

So much for me showing some self-control as a parent.

Beth deciding to pack her bags in the morning and take Sam to her parents made me feel nauseous.

And so, naturally, as fragile couples do when the unthinkable has suddenly become too real to discuss, we talked that night about something completely different.

We talked about her work, or, rather, what was left of it.

'And he said that almost all of the jobs on the floor will be transferring to Germany.' She was still slurring slightly from the unfamiliar alcohol.

'Germany? Why Germany?'

'You know why. I said this would happen.' She had, but it hadn't stopped me casting my vote to leave, thinking I was doing the right thing for once. When

Beth had found out what I'd done she told me our relationship was over. After weeks of my most pathetic pleading, she grudgingly took me back but it was never quite the same again. Now we were both going to pay the price and she had to point out yet again it was all my fault.

'And you think your job will be one of them?'

She shrugged. 'They definitely want me back to work starting next week. They called again.'

'Even if your job is going? That's crazy.'

'No, in the banking world that's sensible. Keep everyone in the dark until all of the documentation and details of who does what and how it all works is recorded. Then we find out. It could be half, it could be all. It was on the cards when I left to have Sam but it's certain now. A few months of transition then the bank will be pretty much a foreign one. The UK office will be done.'

I didn't really understand what Beth's job involved but I knew full well that the mortgage on the house was one hundred per cent dependent on it. 'You really can't lose the job,' I said.

'You think I don't know that?' she snapped. 'You

want to move to Germany?'

I didn't need to answer that. 'I'm sure it'll be okay.' It sounded feeble.

Beth took a big gulp from her glass.

'Puts a bit of perspective on things here, doesn't it?'

It did.

We sat in silence, watching Sam's face twitch in his sleep.

'I forgot to mention. Arthur said that he thinks he may have worked on number twenty-six years ago,' I said. 'He thinks the family back then had a dog. Big black Labrador.'

'I very much doubt it's the same one that's been barking. What was its name, Cujo?'

'He said they were a weird couple living there.'

'Why does that not surprise me?'

She finished her glass and balanced it precariously on her side table, yawned again and reached over to turn off her light. The street lamp outside lit the room. I had forgotten to draw the curtains.

'I'll do them,' I sighed. I prised himself slowly from Sam's twitching body and quietly padded over to the window.

'There's a man outside,' I said.

'So?'

'Well, he's just standing there, smoking and staring at our house.'

'It's a free country.'

'Actually, I think he's staring at next door. Number twenty-six.'

'Then it's no concern of ours, is it? Draw the curtains. I'm tired.'

But I stayed by the window, transfixed by the stationary smoker. His cigarette had finished but he'd used its dying embers to immediately light the next. You don't see that kind of chain smoking often these days and it reminded me of watching my dad smoke when I was a kid, one cigarette after the other despite my pleas for him to stop.

The man outside was tall and thin, almost gaunt. I couldn't see his face in the dim light from the street as his features were hidden in the shadows. The wind was picking up, the gales they'd forecast had arrived early, but the man didn't appear to be bothered by the gusts as they whipped around him.

'He's not moving,' I muttered.

'Neither are you. Move away or he'll see you.'

I shook my head, snapping from my trance. 'Miles away.' As I reached for the curtains I saw the man lean forward, unsteady, as a coughing fit wracked his body. He didn't look well and for a moment I considered going out to check on him, but then my natural laziness got the better of me and I drew the curtains closed, shutting us from the world outside. I crossed the room and worked my way back under the duvet, taking care not to disturb Sam.

'If he's still there in the morning, you can have a word with him,' said Beth sleepily.

I was tempted to go over to the window and check again. The wind howled and Beth sighed dramatically, warning me off and I decided against it. Best not.

*

'Ben?' She was shaking my shoulder.

'What?' I'd been deeply asleep, probably for the first time in the new house. 'Why are you whispering?'

'Don't move. I think there's someone sitting on my side of the bed.'

My eyes blinked open and I stared hard into the darkness. 'That doesn't make any ... there's nothing there,' I whispered.

'Can't you feel it?'

I couldn't feel anything, but my feet were like ice. 'Why are my feet so cold?' They felt as if all the blood had drained out of them.

'Ben, there's a weight, like someone is sitting at the end of the bed. You must be able to feel it!' I could sense her rising panic. 'Ben, I can't turn. It's pinning me down! I'm scared, Ben!'

It was a dream. It had to be a dream. Was she talking in her sleep?

'What do we do, Ben?'

Or maybe she wasn't.

'I promise you, there's nothing there,' I said. 'Give the covers a kick – you're imagining it.'

'I'm not imagining anything.'

She really thought there was someone there.

'Just kick the duvet. You're probably still pissed. Your feet have just gone to sleep and...'

She was definitely awake now and kicked, hard, the covers flying up, the cold air rushing in before she pulled the duvet tight again, scrunching it up in her fists.

Sam, lying between us, didn't move.

'I said it was a dream.'

'It felt real.'

'I didn't feel anything.'

She lay silent for a minute, and then said: 'It's very dark. Why is it so dark?'

'The light from your radio's gone off,' I said, sitting up and looking around the room. It was unusually quiet, too. 'Maybe a fuse has blown?'

Beth reached over to her radio and pressed its power switch. Nothing.

'Power cut?' she asked.

'But the street lights are still on. More likely a fuse. I'll have a look in the morning.' There was no torch in the bedroom and my phone was downstairs, charging – Beth didn't like having any gadgets in the bedroom with Sam sleeping there, her radio was the only exception. 'I'll need to find the fuse box first. It'll have to wait until morning.'

'I think it's in that cupboard in the basement. My dad said the electrics in an old house could be dodgy.'

Even when he wasn't there her old man's opinion counted more than mine. I shook my head. 'It will have to wait.' I lay down and pulled the duvet around me. Maybe if I said nothing she'd go back to sleep.

We lay back to back, like strangers forced to share a bed, Sam slumbering between us.

But the silence disturbed me. There were no noises at all. No distant rumble of traffic, no dogs (mercifully) or cats or foxes. Nothing. I'd never known that the city night could be so quiet.

Even my old watch was still. That was unusual – it had the loudest tick I'd ever heard. I reached over and picked it up. It had stopped at midnight. I shook it. Dead. Looked like the battery needed replacing.

I was about to say something but Beth's breathing was slow and had deepened. She was asleep again. No point in waking her.

An eternity passed. I wriggled my toes, trying to get some warmth back in them. They were still half frozen and, if anything, they felt as though they were getting even colder. I tried rubbing my feet together but to little effect. Would it wake Beth and Sam if I got up and put yesterday's socks back on? Probably. I decided not to risk it and sighed dramatically.

'The power may have been gone off hours ago,' mumbled Beth. She hadn't quite gone to sleep then. 'What about the freezer?'

'I'm not stumbling around in the dark half-pissed. That's how accidents happen.' It came out as "ackshidents" – I was still slurring my words as if to prove the point. Doing nothing was my best option, as was so often the case. I turned on my side and …

*

I woke with a start. I couldn't even remember drifting off.

I could hear an argument. Distant, like it was in a different house, but loud, a man and woman raging at each other, seemingly ignorant of the hour or their neighbours.

'Can you hear that?' I asked, but Beth's only response was her loud breathing, irregular as she dreamt.

I sat upright, taking care not to disturb Sam. My eyes were slow to adjust to the inky black of the room.

'Bloody hell,' I muttered to myself.

'They're under the floors!' I heard a woman's voice shout, close to hysteria. There was no reply, just the sound of something heavy thrown and smashed against a wall. Our bed shook with the impact. Everything was loud and clear even though it wasn't in our room.

But it was in our house.

This wasn't any neighbour.

It was here.

It was downstairs.

My eyes widened and I swallowed hard. 'Beth,' I said, louder now, and I shook her shoulder.

She didn't move.

'Beth. Wake up.' Calm, Ben. Try to stay calm.

Nothing. She was so deeply asleep. How could she not hear that? Something else was thrown and the bed shook again.

What was happening?

My heart was thudding in my chest and I could hear the blood throbbing in my ears.

What was I going to do?

I could use the light from my phone! Of course – why hadn't I thought of that before?

But then I remembered it was two floors below, down in the kitchen, plugged in and charging.

Shit.

There was more noise from downstairs.

Had we unpacked that old torch and put it under the kitchen sink yet? Or was it in the cupboard under the stairs? Did it have any batteries? I couldn't remember even packing the damn thing. Maybe bloody Beth had packed it? This whole moving and unpacking thing was all blurring like a dream, what I'd done, she'd done, what still needed unpacking, it was all too much to keep a handle on. So much to think about.

But if I could get down the stairs and find the torch or my phone I could see what new madness was going on.

The noise downstairs was, if anything, getting louder and more violent. A man's voice was slurred, his words drunkenly running into each other. The woman's was shrill, hysterical, coloured with profanity. Suddenly, there was a loud crash, like a large piece of furniture falling over. And then …

Nothing.

Silence.

Too quiet.

I sat on the edge of the bed, waiting for them to start again. I held my breath and started counting. Ten, eleven, twelve, like marking the time between a flash of lightning and its rumble of thunder. After a minute I stopped and breathed again, my fingers and cold toes unclenching.

But what had that all been about?

I wouldn't be able to rest until I knew what had happened down there.

It was obviously a dream, I knew I was dreaming. What else could it be? Like Beth with the person sitting on the bed, it was all in my head. A couple fighting in the small hours in my own house? It had to be a dream. But it sounded so real, had been so physical, I'd *felt* the bed move. My senses were too alert, my feet cold, my heart too fast, throat too dry. This was too real not to be happening, even if there was no rational explanation and there couldn't possibly be anyone downstairs.

'Beth?'

Still nothing. At least her breathing had slowed. Bad

dream over, darling?

'I'm going downstairs, Beth. I definitely heard something. I'll be careful,' I whispered.

Neither she nor Sam stirred.

I didn't want to go. My eyes were straining for some comfort in the dark and I realised I was holding my breath again as I listened to the silence.

I couldn't just sit there listening all night. I worked my way from under the covers and swung my legs out of bed, my feet finding the floor. Without the warmth of our duvet the whole room felt cold. Was it too cold for Sam, I wondered? I grabbed Beth's dressing gown from the back of the door again and forced my arms again into its too-narrow sleeves.

Still no noise from downstairs, but it was too quiet. My heart was racing, thudding like it wanted to burst out from my chest. I pulled the gown's cord tight around my stomach, the garment feeling ridiculously small on me.

I padded my way to the bedroom door and opened it, stepping out onto the landing. I tried the light switch. Nothing.

But was that a light I could see downstairs? I blinked

hard. It was very dim but flickering softly. I leaned forward to the top of the stairs, trying to see more.

There *was* a light. It looked like candlelight.

That was impossible.

But then someone sitting on the bed was impossible.

The couple arguing in our house, two floors below, was impossible.

'Just a dream,' I assured myself. 'Just a dream.'

But it felt so real.

And it was already more like a nightmare than a dream.

I edged cautiously to the top of the stairs, the wavering light from below my only guide. I reached out for the bannister, using it for balance and security like an old man unsteady on his feet.

One step. Two. Gingerly testing each stair before shifting my weight. Five. Six. Why was I so scared? It was only a dream. Turning clockwise for the next flight down. Was it my imagination or had the flickering below gone? Ten. Eleven. Twelve. I turned on the halfway landing and the light was briefly there again, before fading and then disappearing.

I paused. Still no noise, just the sound of blood

pounding in my ears.

Maybe I should just forget it and go back to bed?

Two more steps down and the light returned below, blooming briefly then fading again.

No, I had to see what it was and where it was coming from. The light could be a flame and…

Suddenly as I turned on the hall landing I could smell and taste smoke in the air.

Was there a fire?

There was a fire downstairs in our basement!

'Beth!' I shouted as I stumbled down the stairs, throwing caution to the wind, bounding down the steps two at a time and spinning on the final turn of the stairs, taking the last few stairs in one reckless leap and landing hard on my left foot, my ankle twisting. Sharp pain shot up my leg.

There was no light, but the acrid smell of smoke was stronger and I could taste it in my mouth. I peered into the gloom of the kitchen but it was too dark to see anyting. Even the cooker's clock was dark.

The basement's old pine door was shut. I didn't stop to wonder why and grasped at the door knob. It was hot to touch, scalding my palm and fingers. I pulled my hand back, swearing. Stretching the too-short sleeve of the dressing gown over my sore hand I tried again.

It was firmly locked.

I tightened my grip on the knob, making my whole arm tense with the effort. I tried to turn it again.

The fabric slid on the brass but the knob stayed firm.

Then, as I relaxed my grip, I felt it turn by itself, sliding under the cotton of the gown's sleeve.

Suddenly, I wanted it to stay closed. I tightened my fingers around it but still it turned.

I gasped and released it, stepping back openmouthed.

Then the basement door swung open by itself and black plumes of roiling smoke escaped from the room and surrounded me. Instinctively, I covered my mouth with my arm, coughing.

I stepped into the basement and saw a fire in the wall exactly where the fireplace would have once been. Its flames leapt and flickered, soaring high up the broken plaster and loose bricks, the fire's smoke rising to the ceiling before coiling into clouds and making its escape through the open door into the rest of the house.

But there was no heat from it, and the room was cold, the flames ghostly, intangible like a movie projected onto the wall. I stood paralysed, incredulous, unable to believe what I was seeing.

It felt so dreamlike, but also so real.

It was our house but it wasn't our house. I mean, it was the same size and shape as our basement room, obviously it was, but it had an ethereal quality in the dim light cast by the ghostly flames. The shadows breathed in and out in the darker recesses of the room and I could hear a faint skittering sound, like mice running under the floorboards.

The boxes had gone, replaced by an armchair, sofa and old coffee table. I'd seen the room like this before, in a picture somewhere, in …

In that strangers' photo album in the box.

I shuddered and stepped into the room. The air was heavy with cobwebs and I tried to brush them away, flailing my arms as if fending off an unseen attacker.

I could sense movement in the shadows to my right, but when I tried to focus it stilled. I could hear distant screams, a woman's, manic, hysterical.

But I could see no-one.

And then there was another voice and it sounded like it was actually rising from the floor beneath my feet. This voice sounded deeper and throaty: 'He will die here,' it said.

It was the voice I had heard before, on the baby monitor.

'Leave me alone!' a different voice, a woman's, whispered from the shifting shadows on the other side of the room. I gasped, my clenched fist filling my mouth to silence my own scream. An emaciated figure was crawling on the floor towards me. As the fire's ghostly light danced I saw the gaunt, blood-soaked figure, a woman, skeletally thin, her bones and feeble muscles visible under her paper-thin flesh. She reached a hand out to me and I saw long, savage cuts the length of her forearm, thick blood slowly pulsing out of the wounds and dripping lazily down onto the floor and a discarded knife.

'I can't take this anymore,' she said.

I recoiled in horror as the smoke curled around her and hid her again from my view.

My hands were shaking uncontrollably.

What was happening?

It is just a dream, I reminded myself. It can't be real.

I backed towards the door. The impossible fire flared then died abruptly, plunging the room into darkness.

I screamed, backing away, but then the dying woman shifted again and I could hear her struggling towards me. I felt the cold of her fingers brush my bare foot. 'Beth!' I shouted, pulling away in panic and tripping over my feet as I stumbled for the stairs, crashing painfully onto the floor.

There was another noise behind me, a sinister, throaty laugh.

I picked myself up and threw myself through the doorway. I slammed the basement door shut and tried to hold the doorknob firm with all my strength, daring it to open and ...

And then...

Silence.

Nothing. The smell of smoke had gone. The smoke had vanished.

It was as if nothing had happened.

I woke in our bed, sweating, shaking, my heart still racing. Having had its fun, the nightmare was finished.

Fuck that for a game of soldiers.

I snuck off into the spare room, taking with me a spare blanket and pillow from a pile at the foot of our bed. No point in disturbing them.

I curled up on the hard floor and was asleep in seconds.

*

Sam's crying woke me. I couldn't have been asleep for more than ten or fifteen minutes. He was howling like a wild animal.

'Sam!'

I ran into our bedroom then froze, unable to believe what I was seeing.

Beth was flailing on the bed, her arms wildly beating against the mattress, catching Sam across his face. Her body writhed uncontrollably and she shook her head frantically from side to side.

Was she having a fit?

What do you do when someone has a fit?

It was like she was possessed, her limbs thrashing viciously, her mouth snarling and spittle flying.

'Beth! Calm down! Help me! What should I do?'

'Fuck off!' she screamed at me.

I reached over Sam and grabbed Beth's shoulders, one in each hand and pressed down hard, shifting all of my weight to my arms in an effort to still her. 'No! Get off! Get off me, Ben!' she shrieked. God, she was strong, bucking against me. Sam was crying. Beth's head twisted savagely from left to right, her teeth snapping at my forearms. I pressed her down into the mattress harder and she lifted her head, straining her neck, tendons tight and sank her teeth into the flesh of my right arm. The pain was instant and I released her shoulders in the shock, pulling back from her as she reared up beneath me, knocking Sam to the floor.

He stopped crying.

'I said get off!' she screeched and smashed a flailing arm into my face. I heard a loud crack and I reeled back from the impact, shaking my head in amazement. The shock was blinding, my ears were singing. Something started running into my mouth from my nose, dripping on to my chest. My balance was failing me and my vision blurred.

Some fucking dream this, I said to myself as the

darkness descended and the world slipped away.

XIII.

I woke with an unpleasant sour taste in my mouth. I lifted my head and saw that I'd been sick in my sleep. My side of the bed was disgusting.

She'd kill me for sure.

My pillow was cold and damp from vomit. The smell was overpowering and made me retch again but this time my stomach was empty.

I'd woken on my own. Beth must have risen earlier and taken Sam downstairs for his morning feed. Maybe she hadn't seen it so she wouldn't know?

I doubted it. I'd never be so lucky.

'Shit,' I said, looking at the soiled bedding. I'd have to tell her about my nightmare. Would she believe me? Hopefully she would just yawn or laugh and…

She was leaving me. In my just-woken fuzziness I'd forgotten the previous evening's conversation and that she was leaving me and the house, taking Sam with her.

Unless that was part of the dream, too? Everything was so confusing. What was real? What had been my imagination running riot?

And I couldn't shake the feeling that it was all the work of the house and its ghost, the woman who had carved into her own arms, hacking with a bread knife into flesh and muscle and tendons until only death could stop her. What had made her do that?

And was that her voice on the baby monitor that time? It sounded too old, too … I don't know … smoky? Can a voice sound smoky? I shuddered, recalling its pleas. "You are not wanted here"? "Leave"? What was that all about? And Jane at twenty-two had said "Go!"

Or was it just in my head?

Enough. What time was it? I checked my watch, the same one that had stopped at midnight in my dream. Working fine now. 7.20am. It was barely light outside. I clambered off the bed and started pulling back the sheets.

The smell was foul, the mix of regurgitated wine, pizza and bile revolting. Even if Beth hadn't seen the mess when she had woken she'd have certainly smelled it.

I stripped the duvet and pillows, bundled them into the under sheet and dropped it all into an empty

Packers box that was doubling as laundry basket until one of us figured out how to work the new washing machine.

Was there any point in trying to talk her out of leaving? Worth a shot, I guessed.

'Beth?' I called from the doorway.

No reply. I trod wearily down the stairs, my body feeling exhausted and heavy from the restless, traumatic night.

She wasn't there.

Surely she hadn't gone already, without saying goodbye and giving me one last chance to plead and beg and humiliate myself at the altar of Beth the Almighty? How could she be so fucking immature and …

I heard a key being turned in the front door's lock, followed by the inevitable 'Ben!' and the loud slam. She thudded down the stairs. It didn't sound good. She avoided my gaze when she entered the kitchen.

Something was very wrong.

'What's up?' I asked, cautiously.

'He's still there,' she said, barely able to control her anger.

'Who's still there? Still where?'

'A & E. Sam's still in A & E. They want to keep him in for observation.'

'What? Why?'

'You don't remember? You don't fucking remember?'

Sam fell off the bed! It hadn't been a dream or a nightmare – that part had been real!

'He's okay?'

'They think so. Like you care!'

'What?'

'You're disgusting,' she said abruptly. She looked up, her eyes were red. 'You know that? You're a bloody monster.'

'What?'

'What was that all about?'

Not everything last night had been a dream. She'd really had that fit. I'd really had to force her down to calm her and…

'You're going to pretend it didn't happen? I have never, not in all our years, never felt so … so …'

My mouth opened but I had no words.

'You had a fit, a bad dream or …'

'A bad dream? Fucking hell, Ben! You're saying that was down to a bad dream? I have never been so scared in my life! You absolutely terrified me!' Her voice was rising, her anger so obvious. 'No-one has ever done anything like that to me Ben, no-one! And those things you called me, they can't be unsaid.'

'What things?'

'Like you don't remember!'

'I don't. I honestly don't.'

'Calling me … that …' she couldn't bring herself to say the word, 'and if you think it's okay for you to … Sam was there, Ben, he saw you! Or didn't you notice him? Were you so, so lost in the moment that you didn't care?'

I shook my head. I couldn't believe what she was saying.

'What?! Let me guess. You don't "remember"? You don't remember how you pinned me down on the bed and then sent Sam flying and then …' She shuddered.

I staggered back from her, rocking on my feet. 'You were having a fit…'

'A what? A fit? Are you mad? Was that rape, Ben? Were you going to rape me? It sure felt like it!' She pointed at her bare shoulders and I saw dark bruises there and on her arms, faint but they would soon colour and darken. I felt nauseous. I reached out to the wall to steady myself. Rape? Rape?! What was she thinking?

'But I didn't…'

'You think I, what, dreamed it?' Her anger was making her entire body shake.

'You…you must have…' I whispered, realising how pathetic I was sounding.

'Are you serious? Are you fucking serious? I know what happened. I know exactly what happened. And you do, too!'

'We need to go and see Sam,' I said.

'Oh, now you care. Woopy doo, good old you. He's fine at the hospital. They will do some more tests when he wakes up, but the doctor says he looks fine. I've been up half the night. I'm going to the bathroom. I'm going to have a shower. A really, really long shower. And then I'm packing and I will go and collect him. Alone. Then I'm off, going home. To Mum and Dad's. And Sam's coming with me and don't you even dare think of following me or I'll get the police involved.'

'You're serious? But nothing ...' But it had.

'Nothing?? You think this is nothing?' She held her free arm out for me to see and the sight of the bruises made me wince. She slammed her fist into my chest. 'You bastard!' The tears ran down her cheeks, the anger in her voice breaking my heart. She shook her head violently. 'Bastard,' she screamed at me as I staggered back from her punches. 'You fucking bastard!'

Speechless, I sank onto a chair. What had happened? Or, more to the point, what did she think had happened? Had she had a nightmare like mine, so tangible and lifelike it was inseparable from real life? And those bruises? They weren't part of any dream. But she'd had a fit!

Or had she?

What had I done?

I wanted to chase up the stairs after her but held back, uncertain. There was nothing I could say that she would hear. Then I heard the bathroom door slam with such fury I decided I had best let her calm down first before attempting a conversation again.

Which might be never.

I clenched my fists and breathed slowly, drawing the air deep into my lungs, trying to calm myself. My heart was thudding wildly.

This was awful. And I was innocent! I had done absolutely nothing wrong.

Or had I?

It had to be the house! The house and its ghosts didn't want us living there. They wanted us gone and were invading our dreams, poisoning our hearts, forcing us apart, driving us out.

Or driving us mad.

It was the fucking house.

XIV.

'My Uber will be here in three minutes,' Beth said. She was still avoiding my eyes. Her bags were packed. One for her, one for Sam. She was taking my son away. They were both leaving me.

'I thought we didn't like Uber,' I said.

'I do, you don't. Like I care what you like any more. There's enough fucked up in our world right now without your stupid boycotts of companies that actually make life easier. I like Uber. Can you do me one tiny favour and listen out for the Uber?'

'It'll be on your phone and…'

'Fine. You can't be bothered. Why am I not surprised? Thanks for nothing. How many times have I said that since we moved here?'

'You know it's the house, right? There's something in this house that is causing all this,' I said. It sounded ridiculous when I said it out loud but I also knew I was right.

'What?'

'The house. The sleepless nights. The accidents.

Those nightmares. The voices. Us not…'

'What voices? What are you on about? Are you serious?'

'It's this place! I didn't do anything!' I had tried to stay rational but was failing miserably. I needed her to see reason but she just wasn't listening.

'You're pathetic.'

'Can I come with you and see Sam?' I asked. She ignored me.

'You'll call to let me know you got there fine?'

'It's ten minutes. I'll get there fine.'

'Can I ..?'

'No, you can't.' She didn't even know what I was about to ask. She sighed dramatically. 'What you can do though Ben is think about what you did to me, to us, and figure out how it will ever be possible for us to be together again.' She jabbed me in the chest with her finger. 'Do you think you can manage that?'

'This is permanent?'

Her mouth fell open. 'I'll come back when I need the rest of our stuff. And the car. It's sandwiched between two fucking great Range Rovers out there and isn't going anywhere soon.'

'But I didn't do anything!'

She glared at me. 'You know that's not true. You make me sick,' she snarled. 'You're still saying I dreamt it all? Or are we back on your "it was nothing" defence?' Her phone pinged. 'That's my cab. Don't call.'

I swallowed hard and made to grab her but she pulled away and picked up a case. 'Let me take one of those for you,' I said but before I could move she had them both and forced her way past me and through the front door, slamming it shut behind her.

'Beth!'

On the other side of the door I heard her talking to a driver and car doors open then close.

It was too much. I felt my strength desert me and leant against the hall wall for support.

My wife had left me. She was taking my son, too. My little Sam.

Because I'd hurt them. Hurt them both. No dream. For real.

Outside, I heard the Prius sweep away.

My wife had left me.

*

It was later. How much later I wasn't exactly sure. That's the curse of daytime drinking and autumn skies – you lose track completely of the time of day. Mainly it's the drinking though. I wasn't drunk, but I was on my way, taking comfort in a bottle rather than confronting the harsh truth of what had just happened.

It was only temporary. She'd be back.

I stared out of the bedroom window, hoping the cab would reappear. By midday I accepted it wasn't going to happen.

And that man was outside again.

With everything else I'd forgotten about him but he was out there. He possibly hadn't moved since the previous evening for all I knew.

He was still looking in the direction of the house next door. According to the forecast the worst storm imaginable was on its way and dark, menacing clouds had been gathering for much of the morning. Had it rained every day since we had moved in? Bloody felt like it at times. Maybe the weather knew something about us moving to that house that I was just too damned stupid to see for myself.

We weren't wanted in that house. Not me, not Beth, not even Sam.

Two out, one to go.

Whatever was in there wanted us all gone.

Was that man outside anything to do with what was happening to us? The sky rumbled a distant warning and the bedroom window panes vibrated. The man in the street must have heard the thunder but he didn't look up at the sky and appeared to be ignorant of the weather. He was just staring at number twenty-six.

Had he really been out there all night? With that cough?

More to the point, would he remain there when the heavens finally opened? He didn't have an umbrella or coat, just a dark suit. He looked like he was dressed for a funeral.

I waved at him to try to catch his eye. Nothing. He was too enthralled by number twenty-six.

He was unsettling me. I had to speak to him.

I headed downstairs, leaving my empty Peroni bottle on the hall table. 'That'll leave a mark,' scolded

Beth's voice in my head. I didn't care. I walked purposefully through my front door to confront the stranger.

Outside, the sky looked even darker. Rain and wind had been the norm for almost a week and there appeared to be a more serious onslaught on its way.

'Excuse me?' I called to the man, trying to sound helpful and hoping the booze wasn't too obvious in my voice.

No response. I strode down the path to our gate. 'Hello? Excuse me? What do you think you're doing?'

I reached out to tap the man on the arm but withdrew with my fingers just inches from his sleeve. Only then did he acknowledge me.

'I am sorry,' he said, turning to face me and offering a weak smile. 'I was quite lost in my thoughts. I do apologise.'

'You were out here last night, too,' I said. 'What's going on?'

The stranger looked bemused and extended his left arm to check his watch. 'Oh my. It is almost three. I had completely lost track of time.' He spoke slowly and very precisely, his words clipped like those of an

English teacher. He seemed short of breath and his shoulders rose and fell with every breath.

'Not being funny, but are you going to be out here all day? Anything I can help you with? Those clouds are ominous so I wouldn't hang around much longer if I were you.'

'No, no. You are completely right. They do look heavy. I did not realise it was so late. But...' He let the sentence hang in the air.

'Is it something about that house?' I asked. 'Number twenty-six?'

The stranger sighed. 'You could say that. I'm trying to build up the courage to go in. It is my mother's house, and I left under a bit of a cloud a few years ago, so it's quite difficult coming back.' He attempted a smile but there was a dark sadness in his eyes.

'Your mother?' I hadn't expected that. 'I'm sorry but we've only just moved in and...' I decided that now was not the time to mention my own family melodrama of the last few days. 'I have called next door to introduce myself a few times but no-one answers.'

'You live on this street?' he asked, the weary smile slipping from his face. He looked surprised. 'But ...'

'We moved in last week and …'

'I must not delay. I have a key.' The stranger walked briskly to the gate of twenty-six.

'Is your mother deaf or hard of hearing?' I asked. 'Is that why she hasn't answered the door when I've called?'

'She is old,' he said with a sigh and he stopped in his tracks, dropping his shoulders. 'Her situation is a difficult one and I have been away for perhaps too long.'

'And you've returned because ..?'

'Because my health is poor and my time is short. Hence me being here now.' I couldn't recall ever hearing anyone saying "hence" before.

'And your mother lives here alone?'

'My mother is here.'

'I guess that makes you our neighbour? I'm Ben, by the way, Ben Collins.'

'You live next door?'

I nodded.

'But … the voices …' Was it my imagination or did I see a look of fear in his eyes?

'What voices? What are you talking about?'

He shook his head and composed himself. 'My name is Pugh. Forget what I said. I am sorry to have so inconvenienced you but be assured I do not plan on staying long. I am only here for my mother. I cannot even be certain that she will welcome me being here.' He looked up at the front of the house and sighed. 'Too many memories. Too many years. It is probably best that you go now and leave me be. Best I do not prolong this any longer than needs be. I am sorry to have disturbed your day.'

'What voices?' I asked again, casting an eye up at the skies and seeing the grey clouds that had gathered were now black. The sky rumbled again and a few heavy drops of rain splattered on the pavement.

'Best you go,' said Pugh, as cold and humourless as the weather. He stood at the door of twenty-six. 'You could catch your death out here. You should leave.'

And with that, he turned his back on me and entered number twenty-six alone, the door closing quietly behind him.

XV.

"What voices?", I had asked, but I knew full well what he was talking about. I had just wanted him to confirm that I wasn't imagining them.

The weather was shit. The rain finally came and hammered angrily against my windows.

My life was shit. But at least I had enough whisky to numb the pain.

To occupy myself rather than surrender completely to self-pity I spent far too long farting around with Beth's old not-so-flat telly. It already looked ancient with its thick silver frame and tiny 20-inch screen. Maybe I should get us a newer one, I thought.

What with? We had no money. Beth was losing her job.

What us? I had lost my Beth. I should have tried calling her but what was the point? And I was too drunk (and too cowardly) to take the car, so chasing after her was never going to happen. Her dad would have just loved that, his loser of a son-in-law on his doorstep, drenched, pissed, pathetic, pleading with his daughter for forgiveness. God only knew what she'd told her parents about what I'd done.

I gave up with the telly. Nothing on anyway. Never was. Besides, I couldn't even find the remote and the tiny buttons hidden along one edge of the TV did bugger-all. Presumably the remote had been tidied away somewhere, waiting to be discovered at a later date. Beth would know where it was, but Beth of course wasn't around to ask.

Have another drink, Ben.

I fumbled with the controls of our old kitchen radio. I hate radio. Resorting to it was a sure sign that I was approaching peak-frustration. The already half-drained bottle of Teacher's another.

The angry storm was taking it up a notch and starting to take itself more seriously, the wind buffeting the windows and the rain lashing against the glass with almost biblical force. As a child I had enjoyed being indoors during a bad storm, snug and cosy, protected from the elements as the angry gods gave it their all. That night though I just felt vulnerable and lonely, the last man on earth. And by nine o'clock, bored and I guess a little bit scared, I showered and climbed under the safety of the duvet.

I took the bottle with me. It was almost empty and I felt empty, too. My resistance crumbled and I tried calling Beth but her mobile diverted instantly to voice mail. Reluctantly, I tried her parents' phone too, but it just rang and rang before the answerphone picked up and suggested I leave a message. 'Beth. I'm sorry. Please call me,' was all I could manage before the futility of the situation overwhelmed me. I could almost hear her old man laughing as I hung up.

Tomorrow I would take the car and go over there and sort this out once and for all. Too pissed to do it now but …

Tomorrow then, after Beth had some time to reflect and a night's sleep to reconsider what I'd said and see her error and be open to a mature, less emotional, more adult conversation. Our life together, Sam's life with us, was all too important to be trashed by, what? Bad dreams, some spooky shit and a simple misunderstanding or two? Seriously?

I was convinced more than ever it was all about this house. It was that woman who killed herself in the basement. That was it – her restless ghost or spirit or whatever was trying to drive us out and …

Ben. Stop it. You don't even believe in that kind of nonsense. Ghosts? Seriously? That was the drink talking.

Maybe you should write that novel about it.

But there had been something, ever since Beth had signed the paperwork for the mortgage there'd been a change in both of us, now I thought about it. The change in her was all too obvious – her moods had darkened, her temper shortened, her sleep had grown more fretful, our arguments more frequent and volatile. After Sam had been born I'd put it down to Post Natal Depression but maybe it hadn't been that. And maybe there'd been a change in me, too. I'd thought I was just reacting to her but on reflection maybe I wasn't. Maybe I was as much to blame.

Or maybe it had all just been the fucking house?

Given a second chance, would I have done anything differently? Had I put too much stress on her? Just because she earned more than me, did it have to continue that way? Could I have tried harder, swallowed a few of my loftier ambitions to be a writer and found something more lucrative, at least for a few years, rather than taken the easier option, the *easiest* option, of leaving it all to Beth? Pile on that pressure, Ben. What did you expect, you idiot?

These were the things we should have talked about earlier. But no, I had spent the summer months fighting with her bloody father. Well done, Ben. Nice priorities.

But maybe I could fix it, fix everything, if she would just pick up her bloody phone. And I would make the effort, make a real effort this time.

That's what I'd do.

Starting tomorrow.

I drained the last drops of whisky from my glass and refilled it.

*

It was 1am and there was as much chance of me getting to sleep as there was Beth walking through the door and begging my forgiveness.

It wasn't going to happen.

Instead, I was sitting cross-legged on the floor of the second bedroom, Sam's room, the one with that box of that dismembered doll and old photo albums.

I was looking again at the photos. Not our wedding ones – that would be pathetic even for me – no, the album of that couple who had lived in the house before us. Sarah and Frank or Jack or whatever his name was.

I don't know what drew me to it but I couldn't stop thinking about them. Had he left it behind by mistake or was it a warning?

Or had someone, some*thing*, put it there for me to find?

I took another sip from my glass and opened the album again. I'd half expected it to be full of new pictures, different photos from the past of the couple and their now-you-see-him, now-you-don't baby, but it was the same pictures, the same sad, staring eyes. Our house, the same but different.

And that picture taken in our basement …

I felt drawn to it, appalled but fascinated. She looked, if anything, even bloodier, the cuts in her arms more brutal and savage, her eyes so lifeless, the puddle of blood deeper, redder, more …

I quickly turned the page, ashamed of my intrusion into a stranger's tragic life.

There were no more photos. I flicked through blank page after blank page, the story of their unhappy time at twenty-four clearly concluded. Disappointed, I stood and dropped the album back into the box and …

I stopped. There was a small black hardback notebook tucked under some crumpled tissue at the bottom. I picked it up and opened it. "SARAH'S" was written on the opening page in childish, loopy capitals. What was it, a diary? Confession? I flicked through a few pages. The handwriting was neat and patient at first, practical lists of things that needed doing when moving into a new home, much like the lists Beth had written for me and stuck on the fridge door with such glee. Unlike Beth's lists, most lines were crossed out, the tasks completed.

Jack (or whatever his name was) was obviously a better husband than me.

But then I turned a page and the writing was suddenly untidy, obviously written in more of a hurry. It was almost illegible but the heading grabbed me and I slid to the floor as I read.

XVI.

September 15th
THIS HOUSE IS HAUNTED!
Jack thinks I'm mad but I heard voices in the basement last night! They were under the floorboards! I couldn't sleep afterwards. Jack was snoring, too – he's really getting on my nerves!

It was a diary, the most private of confessions, but I couldn't stop reading the dead woman's words. Her experiences were so much like my own in the house; inexplicable noises, torrid nightmares, pictures falling off walls. She wrote at length of her growing impatience with her husband and the heated arguments, how a once loving relationship had quickly deteriorated once they'd moved into the house, the disagreements blowing up into blazing rows at the slightest provocation.

ANOTHER FIGHT!

> *I'm not sure how much more of HIM I can take! It's like everything I say or do just isn't good enough for him!*

She certainly liked her capitals and wild punctuation. I read on, each page striking a familiar chord:

> *Jack stormed out in the middle of dinner tonight. What's with him these days??? I couldn't eat after he'd gone. I'd taken ages getting that meal ready. He came back after midnight pissed out of his head. Fell asleep on the couch. I still haven't spoken to him since. We'll have to mend things before Sis comes 'round at the weekend with that new baby of hers. I hope she doesn't expect me to hold it – can never quite get comfortable with those wriggling little buggers!*

That explained the disappearing baby then – it wasn't hers. And unlike her husband (who I'd never liked the sound of) at least I'd managed to keep the drinking under some level of control. I looked at the glass sitting next to me. Or I had, before Beth left me.

The next page was written in a more manic script, and her words were similarly wild, the exclamation marks punctuating every line:

> *MORE VOICES!*
>
> *These were from the radio! This voice kept saying "Go! Go!" in the background of Steve Wright for hours!*
>
> *I tried talking to that new woman who's moved into number 22 but she's just such a self-centred bitch I couldn't stand to be in her kitchen for more than a few minutes and almost ran out*

I turned the page and things appeared to calm down.

> *Jack's left me. Gone to stay with that shit of a brother of his in Tottenham. Good riddance. I actually threw a pair of his boots at him as he went. Must have looked like something out of EastEnders! Don't care what the neighbours think. Don't see anyone around to be truthful. I'm still not sleeping – the nightmares don't stop. I dreamt I was on fire last night – literally on fire, my skin smoking then crisping and when I woke up I swear I could smell smoke in the air and I had to scratch my arms like crazy, skin itching like really bad sunburn.*

And I have a mouse running amok in the kitchen. Droppings everywhere! At least, I hope there's just the one. And that it's a mouse and not the OTHER THING! I don't want to see another one of those here, not after LAST TIME!

I have decided I'm going to try to find more out about the history of this house. There must be something online or somewhere. Maybe it's been on that "Too Haunted!" telly programme! Wouldn't that be something?

Be careful what you wish for, I thought as I turned the page. Her handwriting changed again, this time she was back to the small, precise script of her earlier lists:

Back from the library and found something VERY INTERESTING in an old edition of the local rag on the microfiche thing (or whatever it's called). From the 90s I think and it was all about this house, or rather this row of houses, 22 down to 30 I think. It said the houses had been empty for years because of THE GHOSTS! It said a local ghost expert had investigated for the current owner who wanted to develop them and turn them into flats and had discovered that the houses were built by a man called Smethwick. He was a wealthy industrialist back in Victorian times who had a factory around here. The article said that there were rumours that there had been some horrible accident at the factory and loads of workers had been killed but Smethwick hushed it all up and buried the bodies in the foundations of these actual houses! I knew it! THERE ARE BODIES UNDER THESE FLOORBOARDS!!!!

The article then said that there were lots of spooky goings-on in the street and word was that the houses were haunted by the ANGRY SPIRITS OF THE DEAD who were unable to rest as they hadn't been given the last rites or buried properly and that anyone spending just a few days in one of the houses fled screaming!
I KNOW THAT FEELING!!

I did too. I had no idea if what the woman had found was even in the slightest bit true, but at one in the morning with the best part of our drinks cabinet sloshing around in me it seemed perfectly plausible to me.

I'd have to show this book to Beth when she came

back – it explained everything. And it wasn't just us – it had happened before, many times before. The spirits didn't want anyone disturbing their rest.

I flipped through the remaining pages. There wasn't much more. Her writing deteriorated into an illegible scrawl, to the point where I could barely read it. The last page simply said, in big, angry capital letters:

ENOUGH!

I shivered when I read that.

At the back of the notebook a single piece of folded A4 had been filed away. It was from a company called Elkingtons Properties and addressed to the woman who had committed suicide in our basement:

> *Dear Mrs Warnock*
>
> *Thank you for your letter enquiring about the properties on Amersham Place formerly owned by Elkingtons. As you correctly state, our company sold the properties over twenty years ago and therefore it has no outstanding commercial interest or any legal liability regarding these houses whatsoever.*

However, as someone with an interest in the supernatural I have over the years taken a personal interest in your property and those adjacent to it and can shed a little light on the houses' history.

The houses were originally built in 1857 by the Smethwick factory owner, Jack Smethwick, as cottages for his local workforce. Before the houses were built the land was classified simply as 'waste land' on drawings of the area. I cannot confirm or deny your suggestion that the houses in question are built on an unmarked mass grave. My apologies.

However, I can confirm that you are not the first owner of number 24 to have experienced a high degree of discomfort and distress at the property. I checked the Land Registry records for numbers 22 -28 Amersham Place this morning and they show a remarkably high turnover of sales for three of the properties. Furthermore it is surprising that each of the sellers appears to have made significant financial loss in disposing of their property each time, regardless of buoyancy of the market when sold.

It is striking that no-one has stayed at any of those addresses on Amersham Place for more than a few months before attempting to sell. That is very unusual, especially in some popular area.

The exception is 26 Amersham Place, which actually has the same owner registered today as it had in 1857, the Pugh family. Obviously, the current occupants will not be the original owners so it appears to have been passed on through the generations over the last century and a half, which is in itself quite remarkable.

Maybe you could continue enquiries by talking to your neighbours.

I'm sorry that I cannot help any further with your research into the history of the property. May I suggest

Blah blah blah. My eyes were suddenly tired and I felt that I had read more than enough for one sleepless night.

So our experiences weren't unique. No-one who owned this house had been happy and there was even possibly some truth in Sarah's suggestion that the house and its neighbours were built on unmarked graves of some sort. I made a mental note to look into that Smethwicks company once I got the bloody internet working – they sounded well dodgy.

But I had an explanation of sorts, ridiculous as it was. I drained my glass, put the diary and letter back into the box and made my way back to bed.

I wasn't happy – how could I possibly be happy? – but at least it was starting to make some kind of sense, as much as anything involving restless spirits and things that went bump in the night could make any sense. It explained the war of words between Beth and me, Sam's restlessness, things falling over, voices on the baby monitor, the temper tantrums, our terrifying nightmares, and somehow, simply just knowing that there was an answer, incredible as it was, was enough, at least at that moment in time.

I was asleep in a matter of minutes.

XVII.

I wasn't sure if it was the shouting or that dog barking again that woke me. That I'd fallen so soundly asleep was surprising. That I was woken by the noise from twenty-six less so. The dog sounded manic, louder than before, barely drawing breath between each bark. A man, presumably Pugh, was yelling 'No! No, you stupid bitch, NO!', angry and frantic. At the dog? At his elderly mother? I couldn't tell.

Not that it mattered.

Whatever was going on next door was nothing to do with me. I had enough on my plate without worrying about that noise from next door.

But I wished they'd shut the sweet Jesus up.

I pulled the duvet up over my head trying to muffle out the racket but on and on it went. The man. The dog. The man again. I couldn't make out much of what he was saying but his anger was all too obvious.

Another house in which the occupants were being driven beyond reason by the spirits from the unmarked graves deep below our floorboards? Nothing would have surprised me.

I tried to be patient, but an hour later I was at the end of my tether. There had been no let up. I threw back the covers, stormed angrily to the wall and hammered on it furiously.

'Shut the fuck up!' I shouted until my throat was raw.

Still the noise from the other side of the wall continued.

Despairing, I tried to hide from it. The pillow-over-the-head trick didn't make any difference. Neither did two pillows. I ferreted around in Beth's bedside drawer and found a pair of old foam ear plugs, "100% guaranteed to keep out the loudest snoring" boasted the packet.

That proved to be a lie.

Nothing worked.

When my alarm ticked around to three I bit the bullet and called the local police station. Fat lot of good that did. I must have woken the officer on duty from a particularly deep mid-shift doze and he wasn't up for helping in any way. 'Have you spoken to them?' he yawned.

'Spoken to who?'

He chuckled. 'Been drinking have we, sir? Your neighbours, of course.'

'It's three in the morning…'

'It's not like you'll be waking them up if it's as bad as you say. I can't send a car out until you've at least had a word yourself, can I?'

I supposed he couldn't. I cut the call and turned the light out again.

Then suddenly both the barking and shouting stopped.

Thank God for that.

And, as I drifted off at last, I heard the dog mournfully howling beyond the wall. I didn't care. I was gone.

*

There was a crash. From downstairs again. I heard this one alright.

Even though it was from two floors below the bedroom windows shook with the impact. Something heavy smashed into something hard. I sat bolt upright.

This was definitely no dream. Something had fallen or been pushed over. My bookcases? Or maybe it was one of those wall cupboards in the kitchen that looked a little too far out from the wall, the screws straining with the weight of the plates and crockery Beth had stupidly piled onto its shelves?

At least next door had fallen silent. Maybe their ghosts were sleeping, too.

I knew that I wouldn't be able to go back to sleep until I'd ventured downstairs to see what this latest disaster was. It was too cold to head down in just my boxer shorts so I yanked on yesterday's jeans and found the SuperDry sweatshirt from the pile of clothes I'd left in our temporary laundry box.

Still bleary eyed I stumbled to the stairs, switching on every light I could find on my way down. I was half asleep, more than half pissed, and twice missed my footing, nearly falling. I swore under my breath 'Bloody idiot. Be careful!' I said aloud.

Beth wouldn't have disagreed.

At the foot of the stairs I turned on the kitchen's lights. They were bright and cruel, the LEDs too white for so late at night. Nothing unusual there: the walls and the cupboards were still securely in place. It was a mess, the remains of my earlier Indian microwave extravaganza still stinking the place out, but that was definitely *my* mess.

Must have been something in the basement room.

Shit.

The door was open. With a growing sense of dread, I reached around the corner of the wall and turned on the light.

Bugger.

The two bookcases had been toppled like giant dominoes, their contents scattered all over the floor, the wood splintered beyond repair. One, the left, had spilled the crystal glasses and decanter I had unpacked only the previous day. There was glass everywhere.

Jesus. What a mess.

But it could wait until morning. I needed to sleep and…

Aha!

There was that little Ben gift I'd bought myself for Christmas, a bottle of 13-year-old Balvenie whisky. I think I've been through enough since Beth had left to justify giving myself an early Chrissie present, a more friendly spirit, if you like.

I tiptoed through the shards of cut glass and picked up my prize. The box had fallen but the bottle inside was undamaged. I grinned, grateful for the smallest of mercies. On my way back upstairs I grabbed a tumbler from a kitchen cupboard, then wearily strode up the stairs, bottle and glass in hand. It seemed to be the perfect time for feeling a bit sorry for myself, even if that was starting to become a bit of a habit.

*

At four the dog started up again.

I sat on the duvet, resting against the pillows, absolutely no pretence of attempting sleep. Just me and my sweet, smoky liquid gold companion.

The storm outside showed no signs of taking it so easy and was having another attempt at getting into the record books.

And still it competed with the noise from next door, the dog so loud you'd think it was in the room with me. Another dog, a different dog was now barking outside, joining the impromptu bark-a-long. This one was more distant, down the street somewhere. It was some comfort to know it wasn't just me having my sleep destroyed. Do dogs always bark during storms? If so, that was news to me, but then I've never been a dog person and …

It just wouldn't stop.

Bloody hell, Pugh…

Enough!

I put my glass down, slipped on some trainers and stomped down the stairs. I grabbed my jacket from the hook and angrily snatched my phone and keys from the hall table, the blood pounding in my ears.

I was beyond sleep now, an angry man on a mission. And tired, too. So, so tired. Tired of the house and the ridiculous ghosts. Tired of Beth. Tired of Pugh and the noise from next door. Tired of all this shit.

I opened the front door and the cold rain struck me full-on in the face, the force of the gale almost knocking me off my feet.

Damn you, Pugh. This was all too much.

I stomped out into the wild weather, slamming the door behind me. Even on the street I could hear that fucking dog. My fists tightened, my anger stoked by the booze in my veins strengthening my resolve. I threw my head back and screamed 'Pugh!' into the sky.

I was a man on a mission and strode purposefully into the street and then turned into the garden next door, stepping over the sodden shit and debris dumped out the front of twenty-six, my anger giving my legs new energy. There were no lights visible in the house. No sign of life again, even though I knew he was in there with his mother. What a surprise. I raised my fist and slammed it furiously on the blue door …

… which swung open …

Stunned, I froze, my fist hovering in mid-air.

It hadn't been locked, just left ajar, the overgrown hedge out front protecting it from the crazy winds.

Then I heard a howl from within and knew I had to do something. Before I had time to even think about what I was doing, I pushed the door open and stepped into the darkness of my neighbour's house.

XVIII.

There was something dead in twenty-six.

The smell of rotting meat was unmistakable and it hit me with the force of a wave, stealing my breath and making me gag and splutter. Instinctively I stepped back out into the rain. I covered my nose with my hand, shut my lips tight and entered again. My stomach lurched in protest and my mouth soured with the sudden tang of bile but that was the least of my problems.

I strode further into the hallway. Everything about this screamed "run, you idiot, RUN!" but for some reason I pressed on.

'Pugh?' I called. No answer. I left the front door open just in case I needed to make a speedy exit. The howling storm winds continued unabated outside but the wind and rain stopped at the doorway and didn't enter the hallway.

Maybe they knew something I was just too stupid to work out for myself.

'Pugh?' I was still furious but the house was eerily

silent once I'd entered. No dog barking or howling. No Pugh shouting, either. It was as if whoever or whatever was in there knew I had arrived and at last had what they wanted. Something was waiting for me and I shuddered and felt a cold trickle of sweat run down my spine.

With only the street lights to help me I felt along the wall for a light switch. I found one, ornate, old fashioned brass rather than plastic, and flipped it down. Nothing. Either the bulb or the power had gone. Most likely both. I reached out to the wall and my hand found old, sticky wallpaper peeling away. The dust and old paste stuck to my wet fingers and palm.

My bravado was rapidly disappearing but for reasons I can't explain I continued into the darkness. At the staircase I stopped. Up or down? 'Pugh!' I called. Nothing. I peered up into the gloom above me. 'Pugh?'

The dog barked in response from above then whined, a deep, mournful sound. Beth had been right: the animal sounded like it was in pain.

I climbed the stairs slowly in the dark. 'It's okay boy,' I said, as much to myself as to the animal. It must have heard my voice getting closer and moaned dolefully in response.

On the landing I found another light switch but this too did nothing. My eyes were still struggling to adjust to the darkness. I could just make out three doors, much like the first floor of my own house. The one at the front would be the main bedroom; the second and third would lead to the smaller rooms. I paused then tried the bedroom door. Its handle was stiff from lack of use but it opened easily enough. I was struck again by stale air as it escaped from the confines of the room.

The air smelled dusty, of mothballs, lavender and faintly of pee, the scents of the elderly and infirm. I heard the dog moan again but couldn't see anything. I edged my way along the wall to the curtains and pulled them open, the dull light from the street barely improving things.

In the gloom I could just make out something moving behind the bed.

Peering over I could see it was the dog. Even in the gloom I could see it was a large black one – a Labrador? I had no idea what breed – but by the sound of its raspy breathing it was close to death. It sounded exhausted from its night-long efforts. Beth would have been in tears but I didn't feel even remotely sympathetic to the hound's plight. Instead, I felt a weight of dread in the pit of my stomach as I looked closer.

It was fidgeting listlessly. And then, as my eyes adjusted to the light, I froze, appalled at what I was seeing. I gasped and my hand rose to my mouth. My knees gave way and I had to steady myself by holding the curtain.

The dog was dead.

And from the smell it appeared that it had been dead for some time.

The movement I had seen had been from dozens of swarming rats feeding off the dog's body, the sharp teeth ripping and tearing at the blood-soaked fur and what remained of its rancid flesh, the rats' bellies were already swollen from their feast.

I doubled over and vomited, more whisky than food. The rats turned, sensing something else to gorge on. I recoiled and stepped out of the room, my feet clumsy and uncertain at the top of the stairs. I struggled to keep my balance as I fled the dog that …

… the dog that had barked and howled …

… but had been dead all along …

I needed to get away. Even what I knew of the house's history didn't explain this. Nothing could.

'Pugh!' I called again into the dark as I stumbled down the stairs, my feet awkward and clumsy.

I wanted to flee, needed to escape, but my movements were suddenly weary. Run! Why couldn't I run?!

And then I heard a voice:

'I'm … down … here …'

It came from below. Was it Pugh? Was he still in the house, maybe down in the basement? Whoever it was his words sounded unsure, scared. 'With … mother,' he said, and I froze on the stairs. I looked down but it was like staring into a dark, bottomless well.

I couldn't move.

But knew that I had to go down.

Down into the unknown.

Down into the darkness.

XIX.

I froze on the stairs when I reached the hallway. The front door was still open, tempting me to leave and run. 'I should go home and find that torch,' I said to myself, trying to justify taking the coward's option, but I wasn't thinking straight and I knew that once I left that house there was no way on earth I would ever return. Could I leave Pugh on his own in there? Too bloody right, I could. Why not? It's not like he was a friend or anything. I owed him nothing. Sure, he was an old man and that cough didn't sound particularly healthy, but he could surely look after himself. He didn't need me, a stranger he'd held the briefest of conversations with, riding to the rescue, if indeed rescuing was what he needed.

The sensible thing would have been for me to turn in that hallway, run out through the front door and just keep going, past my own house, down the street and off into the night.

But me and "sensible" weren't even on speaking terms that night and, inexplicably, I felt compelled to stay. 'Pugh?' I called again, staring down the stairwell into the gloom. I just needed Pugh to say he was alright, that it was okay for me to leave, that …

'Who is it?' The voice was distant, like it was behind a door. It sounded weak and out of breath, the two syllables separated by an unnatural pause. Was he hurt in some way? Or was that coughing fit I'd witnessed when I first saw him the symptom of something serious?

I couldn't leave him alone. Alone, that was, aside from that mother of his. Oh, and the rats. Don't forget all of those bloated vermin, still upstairs finishing off what was left of the dog. He'd have the dog for company, too. Mustn't forget the dog.

Maybe the rats would turn on him or his mother next? I shuddered at the memory of those teeth and the ripping sound of the dog's flesh.

I'd never forget that as long as I lived.

Maybe this was all another dream. Another nightmare. I put my hand on the bannister to steady myself. It felt too real. This was no dream, not this time.

Suddenly, there was a noise from below, jolting me

from my thoughts. It sounded like something had fallen.

'Pugh? Pugh? I'm coming down,' I called into the dark.

There was no reply, just the howl of the wind outside.

I put my foot on the first step down. In the darkness the narrow staircase felt treacherous and I clumsily missed my footing, stumbling down the stairs and crashing into the wall at the bottom, my shoulder and teeth juddering with the impact. It hurt but I'd live.

'Pugh?' I shouted again.

No reply. I rubbed my shoulder.

At the foot of the last flight of stairs was a closed door.

'Pugh?' I whispered. My hand grasped the door's knob but my nerve was failing me. I lifted my hand and knocked timidly on the door.

Silence. I steeled myself and slowly twisted the knob. I felt my throat and chest tighten, my mouth dry and my skin suddenly prickle with a cold sweat.

It's just a room, I told myself. It's just a regular room in a regular house, a house made of bricks and mortar.

Besides, what was it we'd joked about all those months ago? There's no such thing as ghosts?

I didn't believe that any more.

I took a deep breath and stepped into the room.

*

The basement was cold and lightless, the drawn curtains keeping any light from the street to themselves. My hands instinctively reached out for the security of a wall to guide me but I was grasping at air. I took a step and felt something fragile underfoot crack under my weight. The floor was covered in clutter, a ridiculous amount of junk and I was ankle deep in it.

Something shifted in the dark. What was that? I froze, my eyes and ears straining.

I could hear heavy breathing; long, laboured rasps, each breath-taking great effort. My own chest ached hearing it.

Someone was in the room with me but my eyes were struggling in the dark. I knew I wasn't alone. It had to be Pugh. Was his mother there, too?

'Hello?' I said. 'Pugh?'

There was no response at first, but then a weak voice gasped 'Collins? Is that … you?'

'Yes! Where are you? I can't see a thing in here.'

'Why are … you … here?' I found his shortness of breath irritating and I felt my anger rising again.

'Why do you think? Because of all that noise you've been making – it's the middle of the night! The shouting, that dog barking and …'

'The dog! Poor thing. I fear it too is cursed and …' but before he could finish more violent coughing seized him and I heard him gasping for air. I didn't know how to react and stood wavering in the dark, unsure what to do. I took a step towards the noise and tripped on something under my feet. I fell down, landing hard on my hands and knees, something sharp stabbing my shin. I swore under my breath then struggled back onto my feet, hands reaching out blindly in the dark. Pugh's coughing had been replaced by deep, wheezy breathing again. Where was he? My eyes weren't adjusting well to the lack of light and I wasn't sure where I could step without stumbling again.

'Over … here!' he croaked but I had no idea where "here" was. His voice sounded even weaker and …

and then I suddenly remembered I had not only picked up my keys in my furious exit from our house but I'd also pocketed my phone at the same time. I took it out and turned it on. The light from the screen was feeble (I'd never been one for the latest gadgets) but by holding it high I could at last get some idea of where I was.

There was nothing 'normal' about that room. I was standing in the world's largest and most chaotic junk shop. It was larger than I'd thought it would be, the whole basement floor had no visible internal walls and was more like a huge attic than a room. And it was full, as if someone had taken everything from every cupboard, shelf, nook and cranny in the entire house and just dumped it all there. There were stacks of tables, chairs, at least three sofas, chests of drawers, cabinets, dressers, desks, wardrobes, crockery, cutlery, pots and pans, old books and magazines, mirrors, paintings, you name it, it was there, all piled in a chaotic mountain range of junk.

But I couldn't see any sign of Pugh.

'Pugh?'

No reply. Had something happened to him? Had

that last bout of coughing finished him off? And what about this mother of his he claimed was still living in the house? It was in such a state I couldn't believe anyone would be able to survive in such squalor.

'Pugh?'

Using the light from my phone's screen I tried picking my way through disarray around me. It was like wading through one of those landfill sites you see on depressing documentaries. I stumbled over something unseen, buried under a pile of coats. Something caught under my feet and I fell again onto my knees, almost dropping my phone. As my hand reached out seeking support it touched something hard and smooth.

It was a human skull.

I recoiled in horror. My eyes widened and I swallowed hard. It was old but very, very real. No ornament or plastic replica. That was the real deal.

I waved my phone from side to side to see better and saw more bones in the clutter around me, long bones, human bones I guessed, arms, legs, even a broken rib cage, all scattered among the clothing and furnishings like weeds in a field.

'Pugh!' I yelled into the dark, my voice close to hysterical.

Suddenly I saw a movement in the shadows, something slowly waving at me. 'Over … here!'

'Pugh?'

I held my phone up to see him better but he was too far away for a clear view. I struggled to make my way towards him, wading through the clutter around me, my makeshift torch's dim light dancing as I clambered over the jumble of obstacles blocking my path.

It was Pugh. He looked older and more tired than when I'd first met him. It was as if returning to the house even for just a few hours had sapped all of his energy and sucked the life from him. He was sitting on a large mattress in the far corner of the room, a pile of clothes and blankets dumped onto an old misshapen sofa next to him.

Pugh tried to say something but he was so short of breath I couldn't understand his words. I shoved a pile of old curtains and carrier bags to one side and tried to get closer to hear him.

'Collins?'

'Yes, Pugh, it's me. What are you doing down here?

This can't be where your mother lives – it's such a fucking tip! You must be mistaken and ...'

'Of course ... I'm not ... mistaken!' he panted, angrily. 'She's here ... you shouldn't have come ...'

I pointed my phone's light directly at him and he flinched as it lit him, hiding his face with his forearm from the weak glow.

Then, with surprising agility, he grabbed my hand and I was shocked at how tight his grip was, his skeletal fingers digging deep into my skin. For someone who sounded like he was at death's door he was surprisingly strong. I tried to pull away but his hold tightened and I struggled. I struck his hand with the edge of my phone and he finally loosened his grip.

'Where's your mother?' I shouted at him. I'd had enough of his shit. 'And what's with the fucking dog?'

'Mother says she's cold. She's under here.' He nodded at the blankets on the sofa next to him.

'Cold,' croaked a voice. I shivered. That didn't sound like him. Was that ... could Pugh's mother be under there?

The blankets moved. 'Not much longer,' said Pugh, patting the top one tenderly.

I stepped further forward and reached for the top blanket, lifting it delicately then dropped it in horror. At first I thought I was looking at something dead, a rotting naked corpse, but then I noticed the slight rise and fall of its chest and realised I was wrong.

I couldn't be sure though as I couldn't see clearly. I moved closer, holding my phone nearer as I lifted the blanket again. A foul, overpowering smell of shit and decay assaulted my mouth and nose. It was the stench of death. I was too terrified to scream.

I dropped the blanket and stepped back, stumbling away, some glass or china breaking under my feet.

It had once been a woman but her face had been so ravaged by age it was little more than a skull, the skin so paper thin it had torn in places, exposing the bones beneath.

Something was moving in her dark mouth and a fat maggot dribbled out over her toothless black gums and fell from her frayed lips onto the blanket.

Her jaw began to move, the bones creaking from the effort. How could she speak? Surely she was dead – there was no way that woman, that … thing … was still alive?

Her frail eyelids trembled then snapped open and her rheumy yellow eyes bore into me. The air rose in her throat and hissed as it escaped.

Whatever it was trying to say, I really didn't want to hear.

'They won't ... let her die,' said Pugh.

His voice startled me and I stepped back from his mother. 'What? Who's they?' I asked.

'The ghosts. She wouldn't listen to their demands to be left alone and now they torment her by keeping her spirit alive even though her flesh is dying. It's the curse ...'

I stared at Pugh. 'What curse?'

'This house ... these houses ... they are built on the unmarked graves of men and women and children who were robbed of life and cannot rest. They were denied the sanctity of holy burial and their spirits are damned for all eternity. Their pain and fury infect the very fabrics of these houses like a contagion.'

I knew what he was referring too – that diary, the letter from the developer. 'You mean the dead from the factory explosion?'

He stared into my eyes. 'That is ... correct.'

'But that was over a hundred years ago and there's no such thing as …'

'Ghosts?' Pugh managed a sinister smile as he finished my sentence. 'Is that what you think after everything you've seen? If only that were the case. They exist. They lurk deep within these walls, beneath the floorboards, in the very air we are breathing. Their anger poisons and pollutes all who are foolish enough to attempt to live in these houses. You have felt it yourself, I am sure. The sudden annoyance with loved ones? An uncontrollable anger? You have no doubt experienced these even if your time here has been limited. The ghosts want you gone and they will drive you away.'

I shook my head. 'I don't believe you,' I said. But I did.

'No-one stays – some last days, one or two a few weeks even, but all leave eventually, driven away by their madness or forced into violence.'

'My wife and son have left me,' I said, quietly.

He nodded but there was no sympathy in his eyes.

It was all true. It had only been a matter of days for us, barely a week, but what he was describing was so familiar. It hadn't been instant, the moment we walked through the door, but it had been noticeable with both me, Beth and even the sleepless baby Sam.

'But what about your mother? She's lived here for years, hasn't she? And her dog – what's that all about?'

'As I said, my mother refused to listen. They forced her to kill my father. Those were his remains you stumbled over just now. She attempted to choke the life from him years ago in one of her rages but the ghosts ensured his spirit remained even as his flesh rotted.' His breathing was labouring again, but he was determined to talk. 'He was powerless as the rats picked clean his bones. My mother took great delight as she watched him being eaten by the vermin. It was her madness and cruelty that drove me away from here. And now she faces a similar fate, and …' He stopped suddenly and his head lolled forwards.

'Pugh? Are you okay?'

He lifted his head slowly. 'I … I am sorry. They don't want me here and I find it difficult to concentrate and …"

'Do you need a glass of water? Something to drink or…'

'There is nothing here to drink. Or eat. Mother has been beyond such needs for many weeks ...'

He looked at me and even in the dim light I could see his own eyes were dull.

'She is stubborn and she would not be driven out. And in their frustration the ghosts have made real her boast that she will live here forever despite them, live in a rotting body that is all but dead.'

'Like the dog?'

'*Exactly* like the dog. It, too, lives beyond death.'

'What do you mean?' I asked.

'Her own spirit cannot sleep. The ghosts promised she will live forever and they have not lied. She should be dead by now, but her rotting flesh is still warm, her heart still beats. She is living in death.'

I shook my head, unable to comprehend what he was saying. 'You say she has to leave?' I was struggling to understand any of this – it all sounded so ridiculous. The living dead? Seriously? 'I'm leaving,' I said. 'And there's no way on earth I'm taking her anywhere.

He shook his head. 'No. You have to take her. This can't continue. I cannot do it. I will now die here. You need to take her far from here, so far that the power of the bones fades and she can finally rest.'

'I can't…'

'Just take her from here, as far away as you can. That's the only way for her to escape from the curse and …'

'This is crazy!'

'Please.' Pugh was pleading. He grabbed my arm and I tried to pull it back but his strength, again, was surprising.

Too confused to argue, I threw the blanket back over his mother. I couldn't bear to look at her a second longer.

'Be careful,' he said. 'She is very fragile, and if she wakes she will fight you rather than be taken from here. Wrap the blanket around her. Lift her gently.'

I shook my head, unable to believe what I was doing. I pulled the blanket tight around what was left of the woman at twenty-six and felt something snap – a bone? – as I wrapped it around her body as tightly as I could. 'Did you hear that?' I asked. 'I think I broke something!'

'It doesn't matter. Just take her,' said Pugh, his voice apparently gaining strength from my compliance. I took a deep breath and lifted her body from the mattress, my fingers sinking deep into the wool and something else snapped. I screamed and dropped the blanket and its contents.

That woke her.

Putrid air escaped from her mouth. 'No!' it whispered.

'Yes!' demanded Pugh.

Something in Pugh's eyes had me transfixed and I couldn't move. The blankets on the mattress were starting to convulse, she was writhing beneath the wool.

Pugh stared at me.

I tried to gather it up again but couldn't get a firm grip and I stumbled backwards.

The blankets fell away as the movement beneath them became too frantic and I saw a roiling swirl of feasting rats and bugs, swollen and bloody where her stomach had once been, feasting on what was left of the woman.

I screamed. Pugh screamed with me. 'Take her! Take her away from here!' he shouted.

No way! I found my feet and lunged at Pugh, my

hands reaching out but he pulled back from me.

'No!' I shouted

'Yes!'

'I can't. Where would I take her?'

'Far away,' he screamed. 'Just GO!'

They were his last words. His head dropped and he fell forwards, his strength gone.

I stared in disbelief. I shook my head and picked myself up. I stepped as quickly as I could through the junk around me and ran for the door. Without looking behind me I bounded up the stairs, stumbling in my urgent need to get the fuck out of there.

I raced down the hall, hurling myself through the open door out into the waiting storm. I collapsed onto my knees on to the wet paving, my lungs gasping for air in the torrential rain.

I struggled to catch my breath. I looked back to see if anything had followed me out of the house. All I could see was darkness within. And then I heard it.

A ghostly laugh, loud and inhuman, and I knew I hadn't escaped at all.

XX.

She hasn't spoken for three hours. I reach over to the passenger seat and pull the blanket from her face.

The smell is getting worse and again I fight the impulse to vomit.

I test her paper-thin skin with the back of my hand. Still warm. She still lives. We've still not travelled far enough.

Stay strong, Ben.

The fog is getting thicker as I cross the Scottish border, the little Mini making light of the hundreds of miles I've already driven. There's a knocking sound when I shift down the gears that's starting to concern me but I fix my eyes on the road and press on. There's snow on the roads ahead, according to the radio. It can't be much further, surely.

I can't believe I went back in there, back into twenty-six. I'd waited until sunrise and the storm had finally died away and somehow found the courage to go back in and collect her. What a messy job that had been.

I'd even found the torch. The torch and daylight gave me the courage.

But I left the dog. Whatever was in that house could have what was left of the dog. I never liked dogs.

My phone buzzes into life on the dashboard. 'Beth calling' says the tiny screen. I ignore it. How do I explain where I am, what I'm doing, without her thinking me mad?

I sigh and press my foot harder on the accelerator. I glance to my left and I'm repulsed by her face again. I pull the blanket up to conceal her and I hear the air escape her lips, which appears to be as close as she can come to protesting now.

She can't live forever. We'll soon be clear of the curse and the woman will finally be far enough away from twenty-six to surrender to death's embrace.

It can't be more than a few more miles.

I drive on, into the night.

Epilogue

'Have there been any offers?' asks the young woman.

The estate agent smiles, returning his phone to his pocket. 'Offers on number twenty-eight? Not yet, but it is very much a buyer's market,' he says. 'We're very busy with every property on our books at the moment. There's another couple scheduled to see this house at two so we'll have to be quick. Busy busy busy this weekend. It's a highly sought-after area.'

'Why are they selling?' she asks.

'He's got a new job overseas or something. At least, that's what I understand.'

She nods but her husband looks sceptical. 'Someone from your office was trying to convince me this morning that it's a sellers' market at this time of year.'

He isn't fazed. 'It's both. Just a very dynamic market at the moment. Good for both sides,' he lies with ease.

'Not sure I believe you, Tim.'

'It's Tom,' says the agent, and he opens the newly-painted door to twenty-eight and leads the couple into the hallway of their dream house.

Acknowledgements

My thanks to our friend Tina Pugh, whose own ghostly experiences inspired me to write a haunted house tale. Tina is also my trusted 'first reader' and her honest feedback on a very poor early draft helped me clarify the story I was trying to tell and complete the book you have just read. Thanks again, Mrs P.

Thanks also to Graeme Elkington, Kev Lamb and Paul Price, early readers of later drafts who helped me over the finishing line.

And finally, love and thanks as always to Jen, not just for her eye-catching cover design but also for her invaluable comments and edits as I wrestled with the final draft.

Also by Neil Bailey and available on Amazon

When She Was Bad

SHORTLISTED FOR THE 2018 'WRITE HERE RIGHT NOW' PRIZE

Life was passing 25-year-old Claire MacDonald by. Okay, so she had a steady office job (but paying barely minimum wage), a too-perfect steady boyfriend (a 'keeper', as Mum constantly reminded her) and a roof over her head (albeit in Deptford), but surely there had to be more in life for her than that? Then she found a bag, an expensive Prada rucksack abandoned at Waterloo station. She couldn't believe her luck. Not just expensive but ridiculously so, a little ray of luxury on that cold winter morning. And she'd been looking for a new bag and the overdraft was growing out of control.
So she took it.
And, once she'd met the bag's owner, the enigmatic Barclay, Claire's predictable, routine life became more thrilling and deadlier than she had ever dreamed it could be as she embarked on a career as the getaway driver for a man seemingly out of control.

Also by Neil Bailey and available on Amazon

Bad For Good

THE SEQUEL TO THE ACCLAIMED WHEN SHE WAS BAD *(SHORTLISTED FOR THE 2018 'WRITE HERE, RIGHT NOW' PRIZE)*

It had been fun. It had been dangerous. But it was no longer fun and it had become far too dangerous. Claire MacDonald's life as a getaway driver for the enigmatic Barclay and his mountainous bodyguard Thug Number Two was spiralling seriously out of control, and someone was watching their every move...

Welcome back to fun and games with Barclay & MacDonald, an even more perilous world than Claire had ever imagined possible

Barclay & MacDonald, a collection of the first two novels, is also available as a paperback or eBook